HIDDEN IN PLAIN VIEW

Also by Blair S. Walker

Up Jumped The Devil

Don't Believe Your Lying Eyes

HIDDEN IN PLAIN VIEW

A DARRYL BILLUPS MYSTERY

BLAIR S. WALKER

PUBLISHED BY
amazon encore

The characters and events portrayed in this book are fictitious. Any similarity to real persons, living or dead, is coincidental and not intended by the author.

Printed in the United States of America.

Published by AmazonEncore
P.O. Box 400818
Las Vegas, NV 89140

ISBN-13: 9781935597612
ISBN-10: 1935597612

This is for everyone who reached into a pocketbook, wallet, money belt, sock—whatever—and bought this novel. Thank you.

ACKNOWLEDGMENTS

Through word and deed, the following folks have been extremely supportive of my efforts to write fiction.

First and foremost are two strong women who have always been stalwarts, my wife, Felicia, and my mom, Dolores Pierre.

Barbranda Walls, you've consistently been in my corner too, along with Kim and Deborah Moir, Marcellus and Linda Alexander, Jessie Beaton Franklin, David Warden, Craig Rice and the late E. Lynn Harris. I appreciate every last one of you.

Finally, I'd like to thank Terry Goodman for helping to usher me into the Amazon family.

CHAPTER ONE

When it comes to spreading a fog of temporary insanity inside the male brain, few things rival sex. But this time it's my girlfriend's sister who's lost her mind—that's the only way I can explain the ridiculous proposition she just whispered in my ear.

"What's the matter, Darryl Billups, you frigid? Imagine that shit, a frigid brother! Now that's got to be a damned first!" LaToya laughs easily as she tightens her hold on my tie. Her other hand has a death grip on my behind.

Smiling sweetly, LaToya pulls me toward her and smacks her lips. At this point I realize that this simple child might not be joking. This is my punishment for those times I've glanced at LaToya and idly wondered what her shapely pelvis would feel like wriggling under mine.

From the next room comes the sound of rustling bedsheets. LaToya's twin sister, Yolanda—my girlfriend and potential fiancée—is still asleep. In our apartment!

"Look, LaToya, this isn't funny. I don't know what you're trying to prove, but you need to chill," I say in a low voice. "I know you don't want me to call your sister!" Grabbing at her wrists, I pull her hands away and step back.

Arching her unkempt eyebrows, LaToya lets out a snorting laugh. "Go ahead, call her ass," she says with a contemptuous wave. "See if I care. Because me and Sis share *everything*."

I'm halfway tempted to call her bluff and wake Yolanda. But nothing but major-league unpleasantness would flow from that move. And blood is still thicker than water—I don't want to stack LaToya's word against mine. Anyway, LaToya will be out of here and back in Houston in a few days.

It's amazing how two children from the same family, identical twins at that, could be so different. Yolanda has her adventuresome side, but for the most part she's prudent, sensible, responsible. I guess she has to be with a three-year-old son.

But LaToya is the original wild child, someone who dangles over the precipice regularly, just to see if she can pull herself back at the last second. Our little encounter isn't about her finding me irresistible. It's about danger. The only thing that surprises me is that she would contemplate stabbing her own flesh and blood just for an adrenaline rush.

The more I learn about you, Sistergirl, the more you scare me.

Before I'd even met LaToya I suspected she had a loose screw, just from listening to Yolanda talk about her. Now, there's no doubt in my mind.

"Don't judge me," she murmurs, reading my mind. "*Try* me!"

I find this so preposterous, so utterly outrageous, that I can't help myself—I begin to laugh. Loud, too, so Yolanda will get out of bed and see what the commotion is all about.

I hear more rustling and sure enough here comes my sweetie, rounding the corner barefoot, wearing one of my T-shirts and rubbing her eyes. It always freaks me out when

Yolanda and her twin are in the same room together. They make a classic before-and-after shot. Pre- and post-sanity, that is.

Yolanda is my baby, as beautiful a sister as God ever put on the planet. When you love someone they automatically become attractive to you, but Yolanda was already the epitome of fine, with her auburn cold waves, high cheekbones and awesome full lips, before I even knew her name.

LaToya looks like Yolanda, too...on acid. She has the same lithe, willowy frame and long legs. Even the same semi-husky voice. And Yolanda's face, only framed by platinum-blond hair about a tenth of an inch long. Fuzz, really. Each of her ears has been spindled, folded and mutilated with six earrings apiece, and a nose ring juts out of her flared left nostril.

Top that off with another one sprouting from her right eyebrow, and a third in her tongue, and you have a classic beauty—camouflaged by industrial-grade peroxide and several pounds of metal. Why, LaToya, why?

She proudly informed me and Yolanda that she even had her clitoris pierced. We'll have to take her word on that one.

"Hey, baby, hey, Sis. What's so funny?" Yolanda asks, frowning. She can be one evil sistah first thing in the morning. Especially when a bunch of foolishness has awakened her at 9 A.M. on her day off.

I walk over and plant a kiss on my woman's forehead, followed by a hug. I was afraid that life with her and Jamal would grow old pretty fast. But a few months into our big experiment, I'm finding that it's not such a bad arrangement, not bad at all.

"Nothing's funny. LaToya was just telling me one her little jokes before I left for work."

"Really?" Yolanda walks into the kitchen and opens the refrigerator door, yawning. "What was it?"

"Nothin'," LaToya spits out. "Just a little something about an impotent brother. But I couldn't remember the punch line."

"Oh, really?" Yolanda emerges from the refrigerator with a bottle of milk and a bemused expression. "Don't pay my sister no attention, baby," Yolanda says in a sleepy voice. "Not much she won't say or do for shock value."

"So I gathered. Well, I'm gonna leave her here to work her charm on you."

"Okay, babe. Be careful, okay?"

LaToya stands with arms crossed, watching us disdainfully. "Excuse me while I barf. This *Leave It to Beaver/Cosby Show* shit is a little more than I can take." She grins, rummaging through her black rucksack for a cigarette. Neither I nor Yolanda smokes, which is another reason I'll be glad to see LaToya go.

Standing on tiptoe, Yolanda snags a box of cereal from the cupboard, then comes to where I'm standing and gives me another hug. "Don't pay LaToya any attention, she's just jealous. She wants to move beyond meaningless one-night stands, but doesn't know how."

LaToya throws back her head in mock dismay. "Chile, if anybody's jealous of anybody around here, it's you," she purrs. "'Cause my kitty is *wiiild*—it's too damn much for one man. It cannot be domesticated."

I laugh uneasily, eager to head to the *Baltimore Herald* so I can get away from Yolanda's touched-in-the-head sibling. Things are a little too intense around here for me.

"Hey, see you guys later," I say, adjusting my tie. "I'm in the wind. And, LaToya...why don't you tell Yolanda your joke? Maybe she can help you finish it."

Chuckling, I close the door to our apartment and walk outside to my little black Japanese coupe that's at one hundred thousand miles and counting. I shake my head all the way to work, thinking about my encounter with LaToya. Thank you, LaToya, for livening up my morning.

But your bold ass will definitely be on a plane headed to Houston come Saturday. You best believe that.

CHAPTER TWO

Nude, his dead body slouched down in an empty white porcelain bathtub with a Confederate flag decal stuck to his handsome brown face, Darcel Moore reminded Detective Philip Gardner of something. What?

Resting his chin in his hand, oblivious to Baltimore Police Department crime technicians combing through Moore's two-bedroom downtown apartment, Gardner stood in the middle of the bathroom trying to force himself to remember.

The "Mona Lisa"! Moore's expression was frozen somewhere between an enigmatic smile and the tiniest of frowns.

As though the realization that his life was over at thirty-six was a puzzling, mildly vexing riddle. If not to Moore, it certainly was to Gardner and his partner, Detective Scott Donatelli.

Moore's trim, athletic body bore no bruises or puncture wounds and a quick run-through of his apartment yielded no drugs or drug paraphernalia. The burglar alarm was activated and the stereo was still playing the bland tunes of his favorite smooth-jazz station when his wife had discovered him.

And her alibi of having just returned from a business trip to Atlanta checked out.

Usually full of irreverent banter and gallows humor at death scenes, Gardner and Donatelli had little to say inside the dead man's apartment. They had just stumbled across their version of the *New York Times* crossword puzzle and were thoroughly engrossed.

Squatting beside the bathtub, Gardner peered intently at the deceased black man's face.

"What the hell was that loud noise, Pops?" Donatelli laughed, finally breaking the silence. "You cracking walnuts… or were those your old knees?"

"Unnnnhuh, I got your walnuts, all right," Gardner said, poker-faced. Moore's wife could be heard quietly sobbing in the living room. "Your young, dumb ass will get here one day. If you're lucky, that is."

The inch-wide Confederate flag decal was dead center on Moore's forehead, right over the bridge of his nose. The work of someone fastidious and unhurried. A perfectionist.

Moore was sprawled on his back and his legs were bent at the knees and splayed open. The bottom of the tub was soiled. Death had relaxed the muscles controlling his bladder and bowels one final time.

"I guess all men aren't created equal, eh?" Gardner said quietly, gesturing toward Moore's shrunken member. "Jesus, my five-year-old grandson is hung better than that!" Gardner smiled briefly, wondering if Mrs. Moore wasn't secretly crying tears of joy.

"His eyes aren't bloodshot, Scotty, so we can probably rule out strangulation," Gardner said, carefully tugging at a raised corner of the Confederate flag with his latex glove. The last thing Gardner wanted to do was to pull up a chunk of skin.

But there was little danger of that. Moore's wife had spoken to him the previous day and a police physician had estimated time of death at less than twenty-four hours. Meaning Moore's epidermis was still relatively fresh and likely to stay put.

"I've got it," Donatelli said, suddenly snapping his fingers. "Our friend noticed the flag on the side of the tub, slipped, fell in and suffered a coronary."

"Do me a favor, huh, Scotty?"

"What's that?"

"Shut the hell up, okay? I'm trying to think here—I know that's foreign territory for you."

Still squatting on knees that Gardner had to admit were starting to ache, he noticed a light blue, rectangular piece of paper under the bathtub. He grunted and picked up a grocery receipt for a gallon of milk, two granola bars and a mousetrap. Squinting to read the type, Gardner saw the receipt had been generated in a supermarket in West Baltimore two weeks earlier.

The Moores' apartment looked a little too neat for a receipt to go unnoticed on the bathroom floor for more than a day or two.

"Scotty, what do you make of this?" Gardner said, barely touching one corner of the receipt as he held it up in the air.

"These two look like they're into housekeeping—it's like a motel bathroom in here," Donatelli said, opening a plastic evidence bag. "I'm gonna ask the missus if they have mice… or keep Confederate flag decals around."

Darcel Moore's widow confirmed that the couple had neither.

Gardner was snapping off his gloves just as two workers from the medical examiner's meat wagon came to pick up Moore's body, stuff it into a body bag and haul it off for an autopsy.

"Your treat today, Scotty, my man," Gardner said, working a wad of gum that was stale even by his standards. "What's the four-star establishment of the day?"

"How 'bout the McDonald's at Martin Luther King and Pratt Street?"

"Sounds like a winner. Long as you pay."

An exhaustive autopsy found Darcel Moore to have been in perfect health without a trace of drugs in his body. No water was in his lungs, ruling out accidental drowning. Over Gardner's strenuous objections, Moore's death was removed from the active homicide file and classified as death by natural causes.

CHAPTER THREE

I swore I would never return to the *Baltimore Herald.* And I meant it. That's why I quit after helping to put an ignorant neo-Nazi named Mark Dillard behind bars for trying to bomb the NAACP's national headquarters in downtown Baltimore.

But it's like my father, James Billups, always says: Never say never. So here's Darryl Billups pulling into the *Herald*'s employee parking lot on a beautiful, sunny Thursday. Hard as it is to believe, they've made yours truly - Darryl Billups - an assistant editor

A good deal of national—even international—notoriety followed the abortive bombing attempt, and a fair amount of it focused on me. Which led to a number of very interesting job offers. I even heard from that self-impressed Negro at the *Washington Sentinel* who'd sat on my application for months until the NAACP deal put me on the map.

The *Sentinel* offered me a position in one of its southern Maryland bureaus, which I had no problem turning down. Having already reported from the streets of Baltimore, and having broken one of the year's top news stories, why would I want to report from the boonies of southern Maryland? The *Sentinel* is arrogant that way.

I eventually took a job in Manhattan with one of the wire services, Reuters. And a funny thing happened—I discovered I wasn't quite as good as I thought I was. Everything I did with Reuters had to be written and reported under severe deadline pressure. Usually within forty-five minutes, sometimes less. The editors there definitely earned their pay rewriting my stuff.

It was a painful experience, but at least I learned that grinding out story after story in a highly pressurized environment isn't something I excel at. Or necessarily want to do.

I found out something else about myself, too. Namely, that I truly love Yolanda and her son, Jamal. We damn near put Amtrak on firm financial footing with our constant trips back and forth between Baltimore and New York. The time spent with Yolanda was the highlight of an otherwise miserable four months in Manhattan, which didn't go well personally or professionally.

You know how some folks bitch and moan when something isn't going well in their lives, but never do anything about it? Well, that definitely ain't me.

Yolanda was willing to move to New York, but I don't think anyone should uproot themselves to follow anyone, unless a marriage, or something close to it, is involved. Anyway, that wouldn't have addressed my professional problems.

So I returned to the world's biggest country town—Baltimore. It's unpretentious in a hick kind of way, a little on the slow side and unapologetically blue-collar. And I love it. It's home.

The *Baltimore Herald* was clearly tickled to hear from me. They had submitted my NAACP stuff to the Pulitzer Prize panel, and I'm told I came within an eyelash of winning. My New York stint further increased my attractiveness in the *Herald*'s eyes, so they offered me an editor position and a $15,000 raise.

"Yo, man, when are you gonna turn me on to your fine sister-in-law?" a voice sings out behind me as I walk toward the front entrance of the *Herald*. I just smile, not even bothering to turn around. That could only be John "Mad Dawg" Murdoch, a *Herald* sportswriter who's my main man.

"Whazzup, brother?" I reply, turning to face Mad Dawg, whose long legs have already put him by my side. The black-and-gold dreadlocks he was "experimenting" with ten months ago still ring his head, only now they're at least a foot in length.

Even though the paper has no official dress code for reporters, the powers that be would love to see Mad Dawg shorn. His dreads have been deemed unprofessional, if not a touch threatening. But in these politically correct times no white editor wants to appear racist by asking Dawg to change his hairstyle. Since I'm part of management now, they quietly asked me if I would do it, but I refused.

For one thing, he doesn't work in my department. Second, I came back to the *Herald* to manage all kinds of reporters, not just be a policeman/Big Brother figure to the black ones. I did casually mention to Mad Dawg the consternation his hair was causing, though, and we had a good laugh about it.

"First of all," I begin, wagging my finger at Dawg like he's an errant child, "I'm not married. You have to be married to have in-laws. See any rings on these fingers?"

"What you want, brotherman?" Dawg says in a pleading, hurt voice. "For me to beg? Nothing but juice in your world, and you can't give your boy a couple of drops?"

Stopping just short of the door, I grab Mad Dawg by his shoulders.

"Man, what did I tell you about LaToya?" I ask, laughing. "Didn't I say that she's crazy? And not like a fox, but like I-N-S-A-N-E! Now, go on about your business while you still have half a mind to do it with. Git!"

A couple of days ago, Mad Dawg spotted me, Yolanda, LaToya and Jamal together at a shopping mall. Of course, LaToya was wearing one her skimpy, freakazoid outfits that always have her buns half hanging out. To my everlasting regret, because Mad Dawg has been inquiring about LaToya like a broken record ever since.

I start to tell him about this morning, but stop short at the last second. Mad Dawg is one of those people who just don't know when to let things drop.

"Well, you know how the old saying goes, don't you, bro'? he says, looking at me slyly out of the corner of his eye. "God helps those who help themselves. So since you can't hook a brother up, guess I'll just have to call your place and do it myself."

I just sigh. Sometimes that's all you can do with Mad Dawg. "Hey, man, suit yourself, okay? But just do me one favor."

"Yeah, what's that?"

"Don't come crying to me when she puts you into a mental hospital. 'Cause, Dawg, I ain't hearing it."

We laugh easily, enjoying each other's company before dealing with the madness we know awaits upstairs.

"I know I am not worthy, great newspaper manager, to marry into your lofty family," Mad Dawg says, setting the ornate glass-and-chrome revolving door spinning, "but before all's said and done, I'm gonna *be* your brother-in-law."

And with that he's gone, gliding across the *Herald* lobby toward the elevators. I stay outside for a second longer, watching

Mad Dawg and wondering what size strait jacket they'll fit him with.

"Are you going to go in, or do you plan to stay outside all morning, Darryl?"

Just like that, the positive vibe Dawg left behind is gone. My guard is back up, my mask back on. I turn to see the earnest face of Cornelius Lawrence, King Handkerchief Head himself. I have to admit that he's been a big help since my return, which is a surprise. I'd expected him to go out of his way to make life difficult, once word got out he was no longer the paper's only black assistant editor.Because black folks like him usually battle ferociously to remain the lone speck of pepper in a sea of salt, rather than help lift up other dark faces.

I suspect Cornelius is being nice so he can spring some kind of elaborate trap. So I'm cordial with him, but that's about it. I haven't forgotten how he backstabbed me when I was a reporter here.

"Good morning, Cornelius," I respond, without a trace of the dialect I automatically slip into with Mad Dawg. "I'll be heading upstairs in a few seconds, thanks. See you there."

"Okay, man, see you in a few." Cornelius hesitates, then stands directly in front of me. "You know, Darryl, it's good to have another black face on the management team here," he says haltingly.

Is that so? I don't know what you're up to, pal, I think as I watch Cornelius march eagerly across the lobby in his ludicrous high-water pants. But you definitely ain't getting pulled off my radar screen. Fool me once, shame on you. Fool me twice, shame on me. But you're not getting a second chance.

My grudge-carrying, suspicious side is a legacy of my maternal grandmother. Sometimes I feel like I need to work it. Other times I think it serves me rather well, thank you.

Waiting another moment or two until Cornelius enters the elevator—can't have black reporters thinking that I'm in league with him—I enter the *Herald*. And flash my ID badge to the guard, get on the elevator and push the button for the fifth floor.

I feel energized as the creaky old contraption begins its slow ascent. Supervising the work of reporters and playing a part in directing news coverage at a major newspaper have been fascinating experiences, I still want to manage a paper one day, and being an assistant editor is a significant baby step in that direction.

When I get to my desk, the paperwork from the day before is just where I left it. The little elves who are supposed to come out and take care of stuff like this overnight have failed me again. Lazy suckers.

Searching for my letter opener, I notice the red light on my phone is blinking. I always leave the ringer turned off, because people still call wanting to talk about the NAACP bombing. But I can tell from the way the light is blinking that it's a message, not a call.

A pleasant surprise awaits.

"Hey, mister big-time editor, this is a blast from your past," a strong, clear voice I recognize instantly says. "Phil Gardner here. If you can pull yourself away from work, we need to talk. I'm still with the police department and my pager number is five-five-five-one-seven-eight-three." Click.

Gardner's the cop who helped me take down Mark Dillard. Phil has turned down at least two promotions since then, because they would have yanked him from the streets of Baltimore he loves so well.

He's not one to phone members of the media, not even me, so something big must be up.

I punch his pager digits into the phone and in less than a minute the red light is winking again.

"*Baltimore Herald*, Darryl Billups speaking."

"Well, if it isn't the world-famous journalist," Gardner says brusquely. "I'm in the luxury apartments at 883 North Charles Street. You need to get down here."

"I'm doing fine, Phil, how are you?" I respond, tweaking Gardner about his usual failure to use social niceties. "I can have one of my reporters be there in about—"

"No! I asked for you. Either you or nobody."

Naturally, I'm intrigued. "I'll be there in about fifteen, okay?"

"See you then, hotshot." Click.

Thanks to my quasi-celebrity status around the *Herald*, getting out of the ten o'clock editors' meeting is no problem, especially once I let on that Gardner wants me.

Those old familiar juices are flowing as I dash toward the elevator at breakneck speed. Once a reporter, always a reporter.

CHAPTER FOUR

She lies at the bottom of the beige Jacuzzi tub, arms at her sides as though reposing in a funeral bier. Like that of a mermaid, her long black hair fans around her head, buoyed by an inch or so of water. This poor soul had been a dark-skinned cutie in life, on the petite side and, I'm guessing, in her late thirties or early forties.

Her stomach is pushed out slightly by the gases of decomposition. The smell of death is in the air—not the overpowering stench of rotting flesh, but an unmistakable sickly odor. I had hoped that becoming an editor meant I would never see anything like this again.

It's clear that someone meant to defile this woman and her memory, and they've done so with a simple act: by placing a small Confederate flag on her forehead. I've seen decals like it any number of times at roadside when I drive to North Carolina to visit my grandfather.

In a society awash with symbols, few pack the visceral punch and conjure such deep-rooted pain for African-Americans as that ugly icon of the Confederacy. Why that's so difficult for so many whites to fathom is beyond me. But whoever left this little memento behind understands perfectly.

I stand beside Gardner and his partner, Scott Donatelli, whose hands are encased in latex and who regards me with undisguised suspicion, as though he resents my presence at an active crime scene.

Gardner just stands there chewing, an impassive cow working its cud. And wearing a nondescript blue, wrinkled-ass suit. I'm damn curious why he's called me here, of course, but resist my natural inclination to bombard him with questions. This is his gambit—let him make the first move.

"Come on," Gardner says gruffly, leading me out of the bathroom, through a living room where African art graces every wall and half of Ikea seems to be on display. Walking to the hallway outside the apartment, we pass a young black woman sitting on the couch and wearing a flight attendant's uniform. She's cutting loose great, heaving sobs as a female police officer tries to console her.

Say *something*, Gardner, goddamn you! You know I can't maintain this silence much longer.

"How've you been, Darryl? You're looking good," Gardner says, smiling impishly, knowing full well I'm about to explode. I halfway expect him to suggest we get coffee and Danish next.

"Come on, Phil, come on. Who was that and why is that disgusting flag on her head?"

"I'll get into all that," he says, rubbing his own forehead wearily. "Hold on." Gardner walks back into the apartment and whispers something to Donatelli, who nods gravely. When Gardner returns, he's wincing slightly.

"You all right?"

He belches into his hand and fans the smell away before it reaches me. "Wouldn't you know that twenty-two years into this damn job, I think I'm getting an ulcer! Do you believe that shit? Come on, let's get out of here. We can go to the deli next door and get some coffee."

"And Danish?"

"What?"

"Nothing. Right behind you."

Gardner has always been deliberate and more than a little cautious, particularly when it comes to the press. This morning marks the first time he's ever called me for anything. Because I sense a big fish on the line, I'll go with the flow and act as if I have nothing pressing to do. Like my job at the *Herald.*

"So how's life in celebrity land?" Gardner asks in the elevator, still maddeningly off topic.

"It's all right. I could do without it, though," I respond, tiring of his little dance. "No question that things have been different since Dillard."

"Tell me about it," Gardner says, suddenly fascinated by his wristwatch. "I could probably be heading Homicide by now, but that's not me. I'm a creature of the streets, I guess."

"So I heard."

We don't say anything else until we enter the deli, with me holding the door open for him. Age before beauty. I don't want any coffee, because I had a cup before I left home and more than one per day makes me jumpy. All I want is the secret this cagey police detective is tantalizing me with.

We sit down at a table where someone has apparently spilled half a cup of coffee. Gardner appears not to notice as he digs in his left jacket pocket and pulls out a little plastic package. It contains three Confederate flag decals similar to the one I saw on that unfortunate woman a few minutes ago. The flags have a white, metal-flake inlay that twinkles in the sunlight.

"I see those things all the time in Virginia and North Carolina," I volunteer.

"Virginia and North Carolina, hell! You can find them in at least twenty-three stores here in Maryland, and five in the District of Columbia."

If he knows that much about those hideous little things... "Then this morning wasn't the first time you've seen one of these on a black corpse, was it?"

"Bingo, Darryl," Gardner says with a grim smile. "Move to the head of the class." He takes a sip of steaming coffee and immediately clutches his stomach as I watch with fascination. Philip Gardner is a queer, complex little man. A damned good cop, but a strange bird.

"If you know that stuff hurts your stomach," I begin slowly, "then why do you keep drinking it?"

"Because, my friend," he says, taking another sip and going through the same routine again, "it hurts so damn good. That woman upstairs is Margaret Cooper, a real estate agent. Her apartment was locked, no signs of forced entry."

"What about the first victim?"

"Guy named Darcel Moore. Same kind of flag, an apartment, no forced entry. We couldn't lift a single strange fingerprint and we dusted the hell outta that place. And get this—the medical examiner couldn't find a cause of death."

"So you think there's a sickie on the loose?"

"I know it."

"Even though there was no cause of death on the first one?"

Gardner just nods. I've known him for a little over five years, and this morning I'm picking up something in the wily cop's face and demeanor I've never noticed before—worry. Maybe that's too strong a word. *Concern* might be better.

"I don't get a good feeling about this," Gardner says absently, as though to himself. "I've been at this long enough that my sixth sense tells me we're not going to find anything with this Cooper lady, either. Don't ask me why…I should be home playing with my grandkids. I already missed my own three grow up."

This wistful, contemplative side is new. I thought he lived, slept and breathed law enforcement work. Guess there was a human being hiding in there all along.

I've idly wondered in the past if he had a private life, and what kind of woman his wife is. Because I don't know too many sisters who let their men come out of the house wearing the wrinkled garments Gardner is usually sporting.

"Why haven't I heard anything about Darcel Moore?"

"Do you know how many dead bodies are removed from houses every day, Darryl? Too many to mention."

"With Confederate flags on their heads and no apparent cause of death?"

Gardner is staring longingly at his empty coffee cup.

"Sure you don't want anything?" he asks, signaling for the waitress.

I really should get back to the *Herald* for the morning editors' meeting. But I'm enjoying sitting here with Gardner, being back on the street. Maybe I left reporting a little too soon.

"She could bring me a hot tea, thanks." Gardner orders my tea, along with another coffee for himself. When he sees my baffled expression, he just puts his finger to his lips and grins. Using a ballpoint to stir cream and sugar into his coffee, which strikes me as unsanitary, Gardner suddenly leans toward me.

"The reason you didn't hear anything about Moore's death is because the reports were pulled so the press wouldn't see them. Higher-ups at the police department thought that if his death made it to the media, you emotional black folk might burn the city down."

"So this is where your friendly neighborhood newspaperman enters the picture?"

"Give yourself a gold star," Gardner says, pulling several folded sheets of paper from one of his vest pockets. I unfold them and see they're police and medical examiner's reports on Darcel Moore.

"I'm gonna put one of my reporters on it right away. You realize I'm gonna run with this as soon as I get back to the paper?"

"No!" Gardner says, bringing his cup and saucer down on the table with a clatter and prompting two other patrons to glance up from their papers. "Don't bring some strange reporter into this, because I ain't talking to him. It's bad enough having to deal with you guys as it is! And hold off at least two days, until we can get a full report on the cause of Cooper's death."

"Can't make you any promises, Phil. First of all, I'm not in the reporter business anymore. Second, how many reporters do you know who give their word regarding when a story will or won't run? I'll try to hold it at least twenty-four hours, though—if I can."

I'm a little surprised at Gardner's naivete. I know how his business works, but he knows surprisingly little about the rules of mine. I guess he feels he knows what he really needs to, namely, that the press is an unpredictable beast that's occasionally useful.

Gardner brings his hand up to his mouth to belch and when he brings it back, I'm stunned to see that it's filled with blood.

"What the—"

He's on his feet quickly, but can't make it to the bathroom before two spurts of bloody vomit splash onto the black-and-white linoleum floor of the deli.

"Oh, shiiit!" Sinking to his knees in the middle of the floor, Gardner begins frantically patting his pockets, first in his trousers, then in his jacket.

"Are you all right? What are you looking for?" I ask, not quite believing what I'm seeing. The deli manager takes two steps toward us, then runs behind the counter and calls 911. "What are you looking for, Phil?"

At the moment, he's not looking for anything. Cheeks puffed grotesquely, eyes bulging, Gardner is sitting on the floor, retching. I snatch a discarded newspaper from a nearby table and spread it in front of him, whereby he directs a red torrent onto the floor. Then he begins breathing in short, terrifying gasps.

"Paaaauggghhhp, paaaa-"

"Paper? Do you need paper?" Gardner nods and I rip a page from the reporter's notebook I still carry out of habit, then hand him my pen. Despite his obvious distress, he manages to neatly write seven numbers.

"This your wife's phone number?" He nods, and slowly lies on his side. I gingerly lift Gardner to remove his jacket, exposing his gun and shoulder harness. I fold the jacket and place it under his head. At least that will keep his salt-and-pepper hair off the dirty floor.

Not sure what to do next, I gently pat Gardner on the back and begin talking in what I hope is a reassuring voice.

"Just hold on, big man, you're going to be fine. An ambulance should be here any second."

I look at my watch and see that it's ten thirty-five. If an ambulance hasn't appeared by ten-forty, I'm going to stuff Gardner into my car and drive him to the hospital myself. I don't know what's wrong with him, but he's obviously losing a lot of blood, so there isn't much time to waste.

His eyes unexpectedly roll back in his head and his eyelids begin fluttering.

"Hey, man, you've got to stay with me," I say loudly, lightly slapping his cheek. That does it—time to go.

I stand up as two Baltimore City Fire Department paramedics come strolling through the door, calm as can be. They walk directly over to Gardner, and one paramedic starts taking his blood pressure and checking his pulse. The other one establishes an IV tube hooked to a bottle filled with clear fluid.

"Does anyone know this man?"

"Yes," I respond quietly, intently watching the paramedics go about their work. "I know him. His name is Philip Gardner and he's a city homicide detective. He was drinking coffee when he started throwing up blood; then he passed out."

Out of nowhere a stretcher on wheels materializes, then Gardner is on it and the paramedics are pushing him toward the street.

"We're taking him to Ida B. Wells Hospital," one of them shouts to me as they hustle Gardner into their ambulance and take off, siren wailing.

Stunned, I stand on the sidewalk and watch as the ambulance goes three blocks, then makes a right turn. The manager of the deli and its other customers stand outside as well.

Stepping back inside the deli and walking toward the bloodstained table where Gardner and I were sitting uneventfully a few minutes ago, I notice something sparkling. It's the Confederate flag decals.

I peel a couple of tattered dollars out of my wallet and let them flutter to the table, stuff the decals in my pocket and quickly walk out the door.

CHAPTER FIVE

The killer of Darcel Moore and Margaret Cooper laughed as two pregnant women started trading punches on the *Jerry Springer Show*, bumping swollen stomachs like enraged rhinos and even landing a couple of glancing haymakers before show security pulled them apart.

Monday through Friday, the ritual never varied. At 9:50, a bag of buttered microwave popcorn was slipped into the microwave and popped for exactly two minutes. Anything less than two minutes would leave nasty unpopped kernels lurking near the bottom of the bag.

When the clock read 9:56, the phone was taken off the hook. People who weren't Springer fans had a way of rudely calling right in the middle of the show, and then not wanting to get off the phone. Jerry Springer was far more important.

At 9:57, it was time to pour a large glass of orange juice, stopping about half an inch from the top. And not that yucky orange juice made from concentrate, either, but fresh-squeezed Florida orange juice. It cost a little more, but the superior taste justified the cost. And if the previous day had gone well, sometimes a shot of Absolut vodka would be added to the orange juice. Sort of a delayed reward—people were too caught up in instant gratification.

Which was why the orange juice was savored—never guzzled. The glass couldn't be empty before the show went off. That was the rule.

At 9:59, it was time to turn on the television, so it would be warm and getting good reception by the time Springer's show came on. The television guide said it came on at ten, but commercials and teases for other shows always pushed the actual time to 10:02.

And then it was time for the best hour on television. Basically, it was the only place on TV where real people showed up with regularity.

Not hypocrites phonily kissing the air and flashing capped teeth at people they couldn't stand. No, real folks came on Springer's show, punching and cursing their way to resolution, instead of mumbling feel-good, namby-pamby bullshit that meant nothing and satisfied no one.

Every day Springer inspired the killer. Specifically, to make a concerted effort to be more assertive and proactive, instead of lying back and passively enduring the steamrollers life always seemed to dispatch.

As for those people who called Springer trash television, what the hell did they know? Springer was the perfect mediator, a clearly intelligent man, smart enough to have been mayor of Cincinnati. You didn't become mayor of a major U.S. city by being stupid, even though a lot of TV critics mistakenly thought stupid people watched Jerry Springer.

Well, stupid people didn't commit murders that baffled Baltimore City's finest and the medical examiner's office, too.

Even the press was clueless. As if anyone cared that two more black residents of Baltimore were dead.

Moore and Cooper never saw it coming. They had been blinded by their arrogance and narcissism. Which was partially why they had been chosen. Moore was so oblivious, he just quietly died, like it never entered his fucking pea brain that anything, or anyone, could possibly hurt him.

Cooper had realized at the last second what was happening. And she made the mistake of begging and pleading for her life. The more she whined, the more powerful the killer became—powerful enough to crush the city of Baltimore with one fist, it seemed.

Prompting a frenzied masturbation session and two knee-buckling orgasms that had rendered the killer dazed for about one blissful hour. That was really dumb, but damn, it felt good. Mustn't get sloppy, though. That's what got you caught.

And the killer of Darcel Moore and Margaret Cooper had no intention of getting caught, or of stopping—not with the list about one third complete. But a little time would have to be spent underground, to let an already cold trail get even colder. If that were possible.

"Oh, ha, ha, ha, look at those simple women. Knock her on her ass, knock that ignorant, weave-wearing hussy right on her fat ass. Jerry Springer, I love you!"

CHAPTER SIX

Detective Scott Donatelli glares when he sees I've returned to Margaret Cooper's apartment without Phil Gardner. About six feet tall and thin as a rail, Donatelli has a shock of unruly jet-black hair that looks suspiciously longer than department regulations allow. Add a thick goatee and an overall youthful appearance and you have a cop with a street-slick look. As in small-time drug dealer. Or maybe pimp.

"Come quick—Gardner just got sick and they took him to the hospital," I gasp, out of breath from running. "Ida B. Wells Hospital."

"What are you talking about?" Donatelli barks, advancing toward me rapidly as though the bad news is somehow my fault. "Where's my partner?"

"He started throwing up blood in a deli; then he passed out. An ambulance crew picked him up a minute ago."

"Shut this scene down," Donatelli yells at a uniformed cop near the front door. "Nobody comes in here, understand?" Then Gardner's cohort and I go flying down the hall toward the elevator as fast as our legs can carry us.

Clearly shaken, Donatelli runs his hands through his long hair several times and impatiently jabs the elevator button.

"Do you know Gardner's wife?" I ask after the elevator arrives and we're on our way down to the lobby.

"Yeah. Of course I know her," he snaps. "Why?"

I don't know what's up with this brusqueness and hostility, but I'm not having it.

"Hey, look, stop biting my head off. Gardner's a friend of mine and I'm upset, too."

"Sorry, sorry," Donatelli mumbles agitatedly. "Yeah, I know Mrs. Gardner. What's up—do you think he's in danger of dying?"

"I have no idea," I respond gently. "But he went through the trouble of writing down his wife's phone number. I figured it would be better if she heard it coming from you."

Donatelli throws his head back, runs his hands through his hair again and takes a deep breath.

"Of course, of course. Good call. Thanks." The big he-man, gruff cop looks worried enough to burst into tears. I know how he feels.

He drives his police vehicle to Ida B. Wells and I drive my car and we converge on the emergency room at the same time. "I'm looking for police detective Philip Gardner," Donatelli tells the admitting nurse, flashing his badge.

The elderly white woman punches up something on her computer screen. After what seems like three days, she says, "He's in ER number three right now, being worked on."

"What can you tell us?" I blurt out.

"Too early to say, but if you gentlemen have a seat over there," she says, waving toward the packed waiting room, "I'll let you know as soon as I hear something."

Donatelli and I sit in facing chairs, saying nothing, trying not to make eye contact and tensing every time a doctor or nurse comes anywhere near us.

"I'm going to call Mrs. Gardner," Donatelli says, springing up before his chair can even get warm. He still looks dazed. "If you hear anything, I'll be at those phones over there."

"Okay, I'll let you know."

Donatelli seems to have pulled himself together when he gets back. The reality of what's happened has had a chance to register. "Mrs. Gardner was pretty shook up," he tells me quietly. "She's on her way now."

The admitting nurse stands in front of us and we both jump to our feet.

"Mr. Gardner is still unconscious and he's been taken to an operating room for exploratory surgery. A surgeon is going to perform a procedure known as a laparotomy."

"What's that?" I ask anxiously.

"Basically, the doctor will make an incision from Mr. Gardner's breastbone to his navel, then look inside his abdominal cavity to find out where the bleeding is coming from."

"That's not a good sign, is it, ma'am?" Donatelli says in a pessimistic voice.

The nurse grabs his hand and gives it a light squeeze. "It's too early to say, young man. We'll do everything we can. As soon as they tell me what they know, I'll tell you."

In the time it took to get that update, maybe twenty seconds, a young mother with two snot-nosed toddlers has plopped down in my seat.

"I need to call the paper," I tell Donatelli. "I'll be right back."

I phone my immediate boss, metro editor Tom Merriwether, hoping he won't be there so I can just leave a voice-mail message. When I was with the *Herald* as a reporter, Merriwether had it in for me, but now that I'm back as a conquering hero turned editor, he's been quite accommodating.

Merriwether always has been adept at gauging political winds and acting accordingly.

"Hello."

"Hey, Tom. Darryl here—"

"Good of you to call, Darryl. I was beginning to wonder if you were going to bother to return to work," Merriwether says, his tone slightly facetious. A bit of the old Merriwether.

"Tom, I'm calling from the emergency room of Ida B. Wells. It's been an incredible morning. I'll fill you in when I get back."

"Are you okay?"

"Yeah, Tom, I'm fine. Remember Phil Gardner, the detective who helped me take down Mark Dillard? He got sick when I went to see him and it doesn't look good."

"Well, Cornelius Lawrence volunteered to supervise the suburban reporting team in your absence." As if I'm concerned about that right now. Did Merriwether even hear what I said?

"Fine, Tom. I'll be back within a half hour at most."

"See you when you get here."

Cornelius is up to something, I think as I hang up the phone. Whatever.

When I get back to the waiting room, Donatelli is sitting with his head in his hands, ignoring the flurry of activity around him.

"Any word?"

"No" he says, squinting as he looks up at the fluorescent lights framing my face. "Absolutely nothing."

"I'm sure Phil is going to be okay," I say hopefully. "He's a tough old bird."

Donatelli's response is to put his head back in his hands.

"Look, Donatelli, do me a favor." Opening my wallet, I take out one of the fancy new business cards the *Herald* printed up for me. "*Please* call me the minute you hear anything. Would you do that for me?"

"Uh, sure, Billups. Sure thing."

"Do you mind if I have one of your cards, or a number where I can page you?"

Donatelli looks at me like I'm one very irritating gnat. He rises slowly, takes a plastic card holder from his trouser pocket and stiffly hands me a card. Then he sits back down and puts his head back in his hands. End of conversation.

Back at the *Herald*, Merriwether and the other editors are overjoyed to hear about the Confederate flag deaths. They want to attack the story immediately.

I'm fired up, too. But because I want the deaths to stop and whoever's responsible to be brought to justice.

My bosses merely want to collect awards and sell newspapers. If that's what motivates them to do the proper thing, so be it.

As the day goes by, I repeatedly find myself going through the motions, giving directions to reporters and immediately forgetting what we just discussed. All I can see is Gardner lying prone on the floor, surrounded by bright red splotches of his blood. And I keep seeing Margaret Cooper, silently beckoning me to do something, *anything*, to catch her killer.

I hope the phone will ring with an update. But Donatelli never does call, so I periodically ring up the hospital's intensive care unit, seeking information. Finally at 3 P.M., nearly four hours after Gardner entered the hospital, I get something definitive: He's in a recovery room and in critical condition following three hours of surgery.

Seems Gardner had a perforated ulcer and needed three pints of blood. Thank you, God, for sparing him. I'll swing by the hospital on my way home from work.

But first I need to tell the brain trust at the *Herald* about a decision I've made.

Tom Merriwether and managing editor Walter Watkins look baffled when I stop by Watkins's office for an impromptu meeting.

"What's on your mind, Darryl?" Watkins wants to know, teeth clamped around a trademark unlit cigar.

"Mr. Watkins, we have some very capable reporters on the metro staff, as you know," I begin. "But I think I should report the Confederate flag story personally, given my relationship with the primary detective on the case. Plus, the Mark Dillard story has given me useful contacts and sources it would take weeks, if not months, for a reporter to build. We need to hit the ground running—it wouldn't surprise me if the *Tribune* was sniffing around this thing right now."

Mentioning the *Herald*'s archrival newspaper, the *Baltimore Tribune*, is a sure way to get attention around here.

"What about the fact that you're an editor here now, Darryl?" Merriwether chimes in.

"Don't get me wrong, I enjoy editing," I reply carefully. "I was thinking that after we follow this Confederate flag thing to its conclusion, I could return to my editing responsibilities. In fact, I would look forward to that."

Watkins smiles. "We'll farm your responsibilities out to Cornelius Lawrence. He's a team player."

I laugh, still pleasantly surprised by my newfound clout. And because Cornelius will surely be overjoyed to discover he has to do his job and mine, too.

CHAPTER SEVEN

"Phil Gardner! How did you know they wouldn't be able to find out what killed Margaret Cooper? How did you know that, you crusty old son of a gun?"

Philip Gardner doesn't respond to my question, which can barely be heard over the beeping, clicking hospital machinery in his room. He's blissfully unaware of me or of anything else right now as he sleeps off the last vestiges of general anesthesia in his body. Crisscrossed with tubing and surgical tape, Gardner seems hopelessly small in his big hospital bed.

It's a safe bet he won't be quaffing his cherished French vanilla coffee beans any time soon.

A formal autopsy is scheduled for Cooper tomorrow, but thus far the medical examiner's office is stumped. They did look for evidence of hypodermic punctures, even examined between Cooper's toes, but that didn't turn up anything.

The one person I would give anything to talk to about this baffling state of affairs, would love to brainstorm with, is off in some postoperative netherworld.

"Come on, Phil," I mutter, frowning. "You knew they wouldn't find a cause of death. So how the hell did Cooper and Moore die? What's your theory?" Gardner's eyes roll lazily under his eyelids, but don't open.

"Sir, I'm sorry, but visiting hours are now over," a nurse says quietly. I was so engrossed in thought that I didn't hear her enter.

"Huh? Oh, yeah, right. I'll be out in a second." She fiddles with the tubing on the IV bag attached to Gardner's left arm, then turns toward the door.

"Nurse!"

"Yes?"

"Does that big tube have to be up his nose? Sure doesn't look very comfortable."

Looking relieved to have a break in her routine, the nurse gives me a bemused look. She's a middle-aged brunette with very close-cropped hair and white ripple soles. I haven't seen a pair of ripple soles since elementary school.

"We're not out to torture Mr. Gardner," she says lightly. "He's pretty well sedated right now, so it's not going to bother him. That's a nasogastric tube to drain his stomach. Mr. Gardner's intestinal tract won't be operating properly for the next couple of days, so he needs to have that tube until his bowels start working."

"How soon will he be out of here?"

"Well, we're talking about some pretty major surgery. Mr. Gardner had part of his stomach removed. It'll be at least four days before he can eat or drink anything. And the earliest he can leave the hospital is in a week."

"Is he going to be okay?"

"He came through the surgery very well," she answers without hesitation. "And he's doing great now, even though it may not look that way to you." Cupping her hands like she's in an Allstate commercial, the nurse smiles. "He's in good hands," she says, then walks out of the room.

Alone with my buddy once again, I walk to the side of Gardner's bed and lean over so my mouth is beside his ear. His face is covered with black-and-gray stubble.

"Hey, man, you need to hurry up and get your gold-bricking ass out of this bed," I say in a firm voice. "Because we've got a bad guy to catch. Anyway, you owe me for that cup of coffee you didn't pay for this morning. See you tomorrow, okay?"

Gardner, who's probably pursuing murder suspects in dreamland, doesn't respond.

On my way out of the hospital, I stop in a lobby rest room. Standing at one of the sinks, I let warm water cascade over both hands, then squirt out a generous mound of pink soap. Rubbing my hands slowly till they're covered with pink film, which I work under my fingernails, I then rinse carefully. The vanquished TB, meningitis and flu germs swirl down the sink.

I'm thirty-three and have never left a hospital without washing my hands. Ain't gonna start tonight, either. On my way out I carefully fold a paper towel and use it to pull open the rest-room door. I have seen too many men merrily fly out of toilet stalls, pass the sink and sail out the door.

When I really have a lot on my mind, I don't turn on the car radio when I drive. So silence accompanies me to West Baltimore, where me and Yolanda are renting a small three-bedroom house. A mental checklist of the next day's tasks starts to take shape.

For one thing, I'm an ink-stained wretch once again, not an editor. So I will come to the *Herald* an hour later than usual.

No, scratch that. I'll call Donatelli first thing in the morning and see if he's agreeable to a little chat.

I need to feel him out, because right now I'm getting an adversarial vibe. We need to do a one-on-one somewhere away from police headquarters so he can see I don't have horns. And that we can be of assistance to each other.

Cops are naturally clannish and suspicious, but I think I can win Donatelli over if I can meet with him for about half an hour. Cops tend to be cheap, too, so I'll offer to buy breakfast. Courtesy of the *Herald*, of course.

So that's priority number one for tomorrow.

After I've done that, I need to start collecting string on Moore and Cooper. Just find out as much as I can about them, because I'm sure there's a common thread. Something besides being thirtysomething and black and having foreheads bearing Confederate flags.

A strange car is parked in front of our house when I pull up. A red Italian convertible with a black cloth top and vanity Maryland WHAZZUP license tags. Oh, no!

Mad Dawg's grinning mug is the first thing I see when I walk through the front door. He's seated at the kitchen table directly in front of LaToya, who looks at me accusatorially. She's wearing makeup—a first—that complements a red leather ultra-miniskirt, a black blouse, a red leather vest and what appear to be black patent leather go-go boots.

I'm nobody's slave to fashion—but damn! Can't Yolanda give her twin a tip or two on how to dress? Where does this woman shop!

Dawg, who's obviously tickled to death with himself, has traded in his work duds for a pair of hip stonewashed jeans, a navy-blue-and-red Howard University sweatshirt and tennis shoes.

"Why you buggin', Darryl?" LaToya cries out as I struggle to loosen my tie. As I do so, I'm nearly brought to my knees by an unexpected blow to my left leg. A shrill war cry rings out.

I turn around and see Jamal, who's jumping up and down with excitement. His overgrown, fellow three-year-old is home and he's ready to rumble.

"My man!" I shout, picking him up and holding him over my head. Then I twirl him around four times and set his dizzy butt back on the floor. "Give me five, brotherman!"

In accordance with our routine, Jamal, who's still a bit tipsy, holds out his little right hand for some dap. Still yanking at my tie, I squat down to deal with my buddy. "What's wrong with your aunt, Jamal?"

He shrugs comically, as if to say, 'I'm in the dark, too!' I grab him, finally free of my restricting neckwear. "Jamal, say 'Auntie is touched in the head!'" I solemnly instruct my young charge.

"Auntie touched da head," he repeats innocently. This is followed by peals of laughter from me and Mad Dawg, a puzzled look from Jamal and a mighty scowl from his extraterrestrial aunt.

"Whazzup, boy," I exclaim, standing up and clasping Dawg's hand. "You definitely on the case, ain't you, brother?"

He laughs his ridiculous, 120-decibel Eddie Murphy chuckle. "Well, bro', as you know, I am definitely a connoisseur of beauty," says Dawg, the king of stale pickup lines that somehow manage to work. "When it became obvious you had a Picasso stashed on the premises, I felt duty bound to check it out."

LaToya tee-hees delightedly. I just roll my eyes. "Just remember what I told you, okay?"

"Aw, man, go on."

LaToya cuts her eyes and starts swiveling her graceful neck, as only a sister can. She's still a pretty woman, despite all her piercing. Of course I would never, *ever*, tell her that.

"Dawg tole me what you said," she says, putting her hands on her hips. Then she waits for me to say something, as if I'm supposed to automatically come clean.

"And what was that, m'dear?"

"You know damn well what," she says, laughing. "But lemme tell you something. If anybody's crazy in here," she says, jutting an inch-long chartreuse fingernail in my face, "it's you, with those Bob Dole suits you love to wear!"

Now she and Dawg are the ones laughing uncontrollably.

"That's okay. I may dress like Bob Dole," I say slowly, "but I don't look like I might need Viagra...which is more than I can say for some people. Watch yourself, boy," I warn Dawg dramatically. "She's dangerous."

"Yeah, whatever," LaToya says sassily. "Me and Dawg are going to leave you two squares here to jam to your Lawrence Welk records."

"Where's Yolanda?" I ask, peeling off my shirt as I look for a cold soda in the refrigerator.

"She went to the store to get some dip and stuff," LaToya says, glancing at Dawg as though she could slather him in whipped cream and devour him on the spot. "Some people know how to treat company."

"Well, LaToya," I say teasingly, "whenever I go somewhere where I'm not being treated well, I leave."

With that, LaToya grabs Dawg's hand and tugs at him like she's known him for years. "Come on," she says, looking directly at me. "I have a feeling, Dawg, that you know how to treat a lady."

"Where are you guys headed?"

"Maybe D.C.," Dawg says, sneaking a quick peek at LaToya's behind, which looks like it's about to explode through her tight leather skirt. "Who knows?" He holds out his arm for his hot date and they stride arm in arm toward the front door.

"Do you have a door key?"

"Yes, daddy," comes the smart-ass reply.

"Don't forget tonight's curfew is midnight," I yell just before the front door bangs shut.

Jamal runs to a window and lifts up the blind, watching as his aunt gets into Dawg's car and it pulls off.

"Well, big man, looks like it's you and me tonight," I say, exhaling contentedly as I step out of my suit pants. Goodbye corporate monkey suit, hello real clothes. Walking to the closet in the bedroom Yolanda and I share, I take a hard look at the brown, off-the-rack suit I wore to work. It's definitely not a flashy number. But Bob Dole—come on!

I hear the front door open, then the sound of plastic bags rustling. My baby's back. Yolanda has to pass our bedroom on the way to the kitchen—ambush time! Smiling, I put my finger to my lips and look at Jamal, who mimics me.

Crouching near the bedroom door in my red Jockey shorts, I set my trap. Jamal quietly comes to my side, finger still at his lips. A split second before Yolanda reaches the door, I spring into the hallway and wrap my arms around her.

"BOOOOOO!"

The next sound is that of two grocery bags hitting the floor, along with the splat! of an extra large jar of mayo giving up the ghost.

Jamal brings his hand to his mouth, terror-stricken. "Uh-oh!" I hear a little three-year-old voice gasp.

I bring my hand to my mouth and echo him. "Uh-oh!"

Mom is not amused. "Dammit to hell—didn't I *tell* you to stop scaring me," she says hotly, surveying the gooey beige mess inside what had been a perfectly good bag of groceries. "Why is it that men never, ever grow up? Stop jumping out of corners—I told you I don't like that."

I instantly hold my hands outstretched, palms down, the bad child awaiting discipline. "I sorry," I mumble in a ludicrous little-boy voice. My partner in crime follows my cue.

"I sorry, Mama," he says, looking up at Yolanda, a hopeful expression on his cherubic face.

Desperately wanting to appear stern and uncompromising, she fights the smile starting to crease the corners of her beautiful mouth. Just the opening I was looking for.

I lift Jamal eye level with his mother. "Say I'm sorry again and give Mama a big kiss," I order him, which he does. I follow suit.

"I sorry, Mama," I mumble, kissing Yolanda's cheeks and neck. "I sorry, I soooooo sorry, Mama. Let Daddy make it up to you."

We must be quite a sight—me in my flame-red underwear, as Jamal and I kiss Yolanda, who's laughing hysterically. "Stop, stop it, you two fools." She giggles. "Get away from me—go on!" Her anger dissipated, my woman hugs me and gives me a long tongue kiss.

"I'll take care of this," I say, gesturing toward the mess on the floor.

"I know that's right!" she says, picking up the other grocery bag and marching into the kitchen of our modest little place. It just seemed fitting that if me and Yolanda and Jamal were going to be a family of sorts, we ought to be in a house.

I may be New Age in some respects, like living with Yolanda without a preacher's blessing, but I'm definitely a traditionalist in others. The Billups family—me, my father and mother, Camille, and my brother, James Jr.—before he died in Vietnam—always lived in a house. Small row houses on Baltimore's west side at first, including one so close to the Baltimore City Zoo that I could sometimes hear lions and bears roaring at night.

From the time I turned thirteen, my family lived in a neat, detached two-story that was about ten years old when we moved in. My father always saw to it that his family was surrounded by four well-maintained walls that belonged to us. And my mother made sure the occupants were always well taken care of and never went wanting for anything, including spiritual sustenance.

I think about that as I watch Yolanda float around the kitchen, unpacking groceries as she smiles and shakes her head. If she and I wind up taking the ultimate leap, we'll buy a house. Not that either one of us is trying to rush down that path. We joke about being in "test drive" mode.

Yolanda doesn't know it, but if we keep flowing like this, I may start casing jewelry stores soon.

My woman warms some lasagna for me and joins me at the kitchen table, even though she's eaten already.

"So how was your day?" she asks after I deposit the first forkful of dinner into my face.

I smile, knowing from experience how this exchange will play out. And realizing I have erred by not inquiring about her day first. "It was okay."

That's a man's shorthand for "Things went well today, thanks. I coped with life's vicissitudes, which managed neither to drag me perilously low nor to boost me ridiculously high. Nothing transpired that I care to dredge up and dissect in rigorous detail, not at this moment, anyway. I would prefer to enjoy my lasagna and your company. But thank you very much for asking."

Women seldom accept the shorthand. Life has to be recorded in minute detail on a continuous audio/video loop, then played back—blow by blow—at a moment's notice. But most important, you must discuss how you *felt* about your day, how it affected you emotionally. Translation: "How was your day?" is really an effort to get an emotional snapshot.

I have had a very emotional day, given what happened to Gardner. But the fear and uncertainty his situation conjures in me is not something I want to connect with right now. I'm hoping that my need for privacy will be respected, but I must be dreaming. Yolanda will be hot when she sees a big front-page Confederate flag story tomorrow without my having uttered a word, but I'll deal with that later.

CHAPTER EIGHT

The Killer was curious. How could this be? The Confederate flag deaths managed to become a front-page *Herald* story! Along with a picture of that haughty, phony Margaret Cooper.

A glamour shot, no less, with that damned I'm-too-pretty-for-words smirk. And that teased black hair flying out of her head, like she'd just been electrocuted. Was that supposed to be cute?

With trembling hands, the Confederate flag killer meticulously folded the *Herald* and gently placed it on the bed so that the blasted front page wouldn't show. Just turn the paper over, make the headline and the picture disappear. And then the crimes would disappear, too. And life would return to normal.

The killer smiled grimly. No sense indulging that fantasy. There would be no turning back now. The Rubicon had been crossed when Darcel Moore's chest heaved for a final time and he starting slumping.

Why couldn't the *Herald* mind its own business? This wasn't about some stupid fifteen minutes of fame! This was about settling scores—time to pay the damn piper.

Darcel Moore and Margaret Cooper had asked for this—no, they'd practically *begged* for this. Watching them die had been a hoot. Especially the high-and-mighty Cooper and her shameless sniveling.

She was exactly where she deserved to be—on a cold metal slab wearing a toe tag. Hopefully without the mascara and two inches of makeup she slathered all over her face just to go to the supermarket. Yeah, she was finally reduced to her essence, shorn of the designer duds and the suffocating pretension.

And the truly delicious part was she knew who did it to her. The killer's face had been the last thing she had seen. Definitely poetic justice.

Moore died as he had lived—an arrogant bastard convinced of his immortality. Way too vital to the ebb and flow of the universe to ever wind up taking a dirt nap. But the great lover was sure taking one now, right in Mount Royal Cemetery. Him and his one-inch peter.

That's what you get for underestimating me, for toying with me.

Today's story in the *Herald* would only attract other newspapers and TV stations, like flies to carrion. And the police would be right behind them, because half of Baltimore would be searching for the bold white man who dared to kill black citizen residents, then befoul their corpses with a symbol of the hated Confederacy.

With all the hue and cry and the reporters and homicide detectives tripping over themselves, collectively they might get lucky enough to find the murderer. The killer couldn't have that. Today's *Herald* brought on an uneasy sensation. A sense of being hunted, of being a step ahead of the bloodhounds.

Every cop, every shopping-mall security guard, every knock on a door would be cause for concern from this point forward. Well, so be it. Because Moore and Cooper were definitely gonna have some company.

And that was gonna happen regardless of how long it was necessary to lie low.

Who had written that damned *Herald* story, anyway?

The paper was shaking again when it was lifted from the bed, though not as badly as before. "Darryl Billups, huh?" The reporter who had stopped the NAACP bombing.

"Don't fuck with me, Darryl," the killer mumbled, "or they'll wind up planting your little black ass in the ground, too. Wishing you were in Dixie."

The paper was half folded, half rolled like a paperboy would, then casually tossed across the bedroom. Arcing gracefully, it streaked toward a metal trash can resting against the far wall and scored a bull's-eye without touching the rim.

A lucky shot, given the shaking hands. "Sorry, Jerry Springer, but I need to bump up the schedule a little bit today."

Fetching a glass from the kitchen, the Confederate flag killer filled it with fresh-squeezed Florida orange juice, stopping about half an inch from the top. A shot of Absolut followed, then another.

It was time to leave Baltimore, to take the $895 out of savings and just vanish into thin air. Trudy in Atlanta was always asking when her favorite cousin was coming for a visit. Well, now she was finally going to get her wish. About four weeks' worth.

"Let's see how you like them apples, Darryl Billups. Let's see how smart you really are.

CHAPTER NINE

Take your average cop, make him an instant millionnaire and he'd probably still take most of his meals in some hole-in-the-wall greasy spoon. Like the dive I'm sitting in with Scott Donatelli on Baltimore Street, about two blocks from police headquarters.

A toothpick does a steady 33 rpm in his mouth, capping off his street-thug look. He strokes his goatee in a way that's more impatient than pensive. I suspect the only reason he agreed to meet me this morning is because of my relationship with Gardner.

We have been in this little eatery, where the floor looks as if it was swept two weeks ago, for about five minutes and Donatelli is already two-thirds finished with a huge plate of grits, eggs and sausage I bought him.

I have yet to bite into the glazed donut the waitress brought with my coffee. The hard glint in Donatelli's eye tells me he isn't buying my proposal that we become allies.

I've got the charming, deferential Darryl Billups turned up full blast, only Donatelli isn't biting. He slowly sops his plate with a piece of bread—something I've never seen a white man do before—and keeps his eyes locked on mine.

He's definitely a hard nut, and I can't tell if it's from cynicism, arrogance or both.

Pulling the toothpick from his mouth, the young detective appears almost courtly as he dabs at his mouth with his paper napkin.

I ask him, "So what do you think—does that plan of action make sense to you?"

Pausing for a second, he scratches his chin and looks up at a fan cleaving through bluish-gray ceiling smoke from cooking and cigarettes.

"Lemme put it to you this way, Darryl," Donatelli says, jamming the toothpick home. "If I were to come up to the *Herald* this morning and try to write a story, whaddaya think would happen?"

I know what he wants me to say; I can see where he's going. But I'll be damned if I'm going to make it easy for him. "Well, you could conceivably write a story that wins a Pulitzer," I answer, taking pains to keep my expression neutral so he won't think I'm being a smart-ass. "Because even though you don't have years of training as a journalist, that doesn't foreclose the possibility you may have innate ability."

Donatelli laughs, a first. "You're good, Darryl. But you know damn well the likelihood—the probability—is that I couldn't write my way out of a paper bag. Because you're a pro at what you do, and you have years of training."

Pausing dramatically, he takes the toothpick from his mouth again. "And if I stepped into your newsroom, I would be a dilettante, a fish out of water." He goes back to sopping his plate. I'm starting to form a grudging respect for Donatelli. He must be hell in a one-on-one interrogation.

"The point is, Darryl, homicide investigations aren't a game. You got lucky with that NAACP thing, but tracking killers is for pros. This isn't some Nancy Drew shit we're dealing with here. Not only can you get smoked, but evidence can get tainted and suspects accidentally tipped off if an amateur is in the mix. Which is a long-winded way of saying no. No deal. No, thanks."

Registering no reaction, I pick up my coffee cup and take a slow, deliberate sip. I didn't come to this crowded, smoky little dump to hear "no." "You're absolute right, it's not a game. I have the utmost respect for what you and Phil do...I don't think I could do it myself. But I never proposed running around trying to catch murderers. What I said was, we could help each other by strategically sharing information. We'll both be looking under a lot of rocks, so why reinvent the wheel? If I come across something that could push your investigation forward, I'm more than willing to share it. And if you share something you want me to keep out of the paper, I'll honor that."

Donatelli turns that one over, leaning back in his chair and accidentally bumping into a customer seated at the table behind us. "'Scuse me, miss." Taking a cigarette pack from his jacket pocket, he shakes out a cancer stick. "Ya mind if I smoke?" he says, simultaneously flicking his lighter and firing up.

"Me and Phil worked pretty good as a team," I volunteer, taking advantage of his momentary silence. "His career sure doesn't seem to have been hurt by collaring the NAACP bombers."

Donatelli's frown tells me that I need to have more finesse. "So if I work with you, Darryl, I'll be police commissioner in a couple of months? No, I don't think so. I sort of like working with cops, know what I mean? That's why I became one. And most cops will tell you that the only good reporter is a..."

"Dead one?" I finish with a laugh. "Can I quote you on that?"

"Look, Darryl, you and Phil may have a good relationship. And you guys did a fantastic job with the NAACP. But," he says, glancing up at the ceiling fan again, "I ain't Phil, okay? I'm really honored you would ask me," he adds, giving me a taste of my own flattery routine, "but I don't think so. That's not my style."

Damn.

"Okay, Scott—do you mind if I call you Scott? I can respect that." It's time to back off, but I know I'll come at him again later, and I suspect he does, too. Because homicide detectives and reporters are basically kindred spirits—confidence men in search of the next hot lead.

"So do you have any theories on what killed Moore and Cooper?" That question elicits the dentist-office grimace cops usually wear when reporters are around.

"Hey, Darryl gotta hit the bricks. I'm the one who gets paid to find out who killed who, so I better get moving. Thanks for breakfast." With that he's rising, shaking my hand and moving out the door. Leaving me to deal with rejection and our breakfast check.

Well, at least I know his antipathy is rooted in professional bias and has nothing to do with me personally. Because when you're dealing with white people, you can never really be sure.

So here I sit at square one. The *Herald* has temporarily attached me to its special investigations team. Technically I'm supposed to report to their editor, but Tom Merriwether told me not to bother with that formality and just keep him apprised of how things are going.

I'm essentially a one-man investigations squad, with no time frame to come up with information or stories. But it's understood that in return for that kind of autonomy, I'd better come up with some pretty spectacular stuff. I like the freedom, but also feel the pressure it brings.

My next stop is Hopkins Plaza in downtown Baltimore, where I'm supposed to meet with Darcel Moore's widow in front of the Morris A. Mechanic Theater at ten o'clock, a half hour from now.

CHAPTER TEN

Donita Moore is a full thirty minutes late by the time she strolls up to the Morris Mechanic's ticket window. We had described ourselves to each other over the phone, so I recognize her immediately.

Her appearance is as advertised: She's an ordinary-looking black woman a touch on the scrawny side and wearing a dark, pinstriped pantsuit. Along with a stylish tan hat tilted at a rakish angle, and some cool shades. She has a jaunty, almost feisty demeanor—not the subdued grieving widow.

"I'm so sorry," she says, extending her hand. "I just lost track of time—there's really no excuse." Her handshake is firm and direct.

"Don't even mention it," I say, smiling casually, secretly annoyed at having wasted thirty precious minutes cooling my heels. We walk into a little restaurant off the open-air plaza near the theater.

"Would you like some coffee, maybe an early lunch?"

"I'm not in any rush," she responds. "I own a consulting business, so my time is my own." The widow Moore orders a salad, while I order a soda. Reaching into one of my "Bob

Dole" jackets, I pull out a microcassette tape recorder, turn it on and place in on the table in front of Moore.

"What kind of man was your husband?"

"Darcel was a good person—he was smart, went to church on Sundays. I've never met anyone like him," she says in an unsentimental tone. As we continue talking, I learn that Darcel Moore went to Northwestern High in Baltimore—my school—was working on an M.B.A. at Morgan State University and was a mid-level manager for Baltimore Gas & Electric who had a real estate business on the side.

"Do you have a picture we could run in the paper?"

Donita Moore shakes her head, looking embarrassed. "No, I don't have one in my wallet, but I can certainly send one to the *Herald*."

"We can have a courier run by and pick one up this afternoon, if that's okay with you."

"Fine, fine. No problem. I'll be home after three o'clock."

"Do you know of any reason why someone would want to kill your husband?" I ask gently.

"There were a number of times I could have killed him myself," she says matter-of-factly, catching me off guard. "Darcel had a zipper problem…I know that he loved me, though."

"What were his views on race?"

"Why do you ask that?"

"Well, your husband was found with a Confederate flag on his body. Was he a radical, someone who made waves about race?"

"No, he wasn't a radical by a long shot. He would just as soon run after a snowflake as he would a sister," Moore says, suddenly bitter. She strikes me as sad, but a long way from distraught. "Mr. Billups, could you do me one favor, please?"

"If I can, sure."

"Darcel wasn't perfect, but he didn't deserve to die like this. It's eating up his family that no one knows what happened. If you could shed some light on it, a lot of people would be very grateful."

When our conversation ends, I thank Moore for her time and leave with a somewhat better sense of who Darcel Moore was. An unassuming straight arrow, for the most part, who occasionally allowed himself to fall into what my father politely calls "the tender trap."

Certainly not someone who would be on the Klan's Most Wanted List.

At one-thirty, I stop by Margaret Cooper's apartment to speak with her roommate, Debra Sutton. She's the one I saw crying on the couch yesterday.

When someone opens the door to Cooper's apartment, I'm amazed to see wall-to-wall women, a few of them white. About four or five occupants look so butch their testosterone levels probably surpass mine.

"Hi, I'm Darryl Billups with the *Herald*, and I'm here to see Debra Sutton." The woman who opened the door is a chocolate sweetie with short hair and a beautiful smile. She has a red-and-white apron over her jeans and an insulated cooking mitten on her right hand.

"Come on in,' she says, wiping her forehead and taking off the mitten to shake my hand. "Debra's over here."

Sutton is surrounded by solicitous women trying their best to comfort her. Dark circles surround her eyes, which are red and watery. The air is thick with the odor of jasmine incense.

"You probably don't remember, but I was here yesterday," I say, taking out my tape recorder.

The huskiest of the butch women gets up from the couch and stands directly in front of me. I'm five-foot-ten and she has me by a good five inches.

"Can't you see the woman is emotional right now?" she says, fairly vibrating with menace. "You reporters are like vultures!"

"Come on," I reply mildly. "We both know what time it is—there's no need for those gyrations. I'm just trying to help Miss Sutton find out who killed her roommate."

"It's all right, Sharon," Sutton calls out from the couch. "We already talked over the phone."

Motioning for me to follow her, Sutton walks into the bedroom and closes the door. She looks aghast. "I'm sorry, can I offer you anything to drink?"

"No, thanks. Do you need something yourself before we start talking?"

She shakes her head slowly. "Did you spend the night here last night?" I ask.

"No," she says in a monotone. "I went to a friend's house, but I'm staying here tonight. Marge would have wanted me to. She never ran from a damn thing."

"Aren't you a little concerned for your safety?" I ask in a voice that hints that spending the night may not be a great idea.

"I'll be fine. Just about every woman you saw out there is going to stay here tonight, too. Besides, Marge didn't have an enemy in the world. This is some kind of freak thing—she was just in the wrong place at the wrong time."

Debra Sutton begins to tell me about her late lover, who it turns out was a lesbian with a very successful real estate practice, was a regular playgoer at Center Stage and had a brown belt in tae kwon do. And she loved African violets—I saw at least six when I was here yesterday. She also loved herself some Debra Sutton. They considered themselves married.

Sutton, a flight attendant, was thousands of miles away two days ago, in Paris, around the time the medical examiner estimates Cooper died.

Cooper and Moore both attended Bethel A.M.E, sold real estate and were thirty-six when they died.

Thoroughly baffled, I drive back to the *Herald* to write a story about the lives and mysterious deaths of Darcel Moore and Margaret Cooper.

Philip Alvin Gardner died today at Ida B. Wells Hospital. Around two-thirty in the afternoon, while I was coming back to the *Herald* from Margaret Cooper's apartment. The doctors said a blood clot caused a massive stroke that killed Gardner in less than an hour. The hospital spokesman took pains not to link the blood clot to Gardner's emergency surgery, but postoperative blood clots are an unfortunate fact of life for older patients sometimes.

Not that fifty-four is terribly old.

He was conscious before the stroke took him out, but I didn't get a chance to talk to him. To say goodbye. Knowing him, had he been aware that mere minutes were left, he would have spent them pumping me for information about Moore and Cooper.

I didn't want anyone in the newsroom to see me cry, so I came out to the parking lot and sat in my car. The last time I got sucker-punched like this was when an Army chaplain informed my family that my older brother, James Jr., would be returning from Vietnam in a body bag. I loathed the sight of olive-green dress uniforms for a long time—they dredged up the same pain I feel now.

If it weren't for Jamal, I probably would have observed a quick moment of silence for Gardner and kept working. But I understand now what he must have felt for his grandchildren. And how they must have loved their grandpa.

As I was sitting in my car, thinking about Gardner, something happened that I've never experienced before. I'm not a big believer in paranormal stuff, UFOs and spooks and what not. But there is absolutely no doubt in my mind that Philip Gardner came to my car. I just felt a sudden sense of calm and reassurance. Very peaceful. And I had this odd sensation of momentarily tapping into a reservoir of strength and wisdom outside my own.

It made me want to get out of my car and rush back to the newsroom and throw everything I had at the Moore/Cooper story. Which is exactly what I did. And then, at my insistence, I did something I haven't done in years. I wrote an obituary—Philip Gardner's. In lieu of flowers, I wrote a heartfelt obituary that captured the essence of the man.

That's the proudest I have ever felt of an obit.

I don't believe in laying guilt on people or making them feel indebted. And nothing I saw led me to believe Gardner had, either. But ever since that odd experience in the car, I feel like I owe him something. Like nailing a murderer.

Frankly, I don't know if I can pull that off. But I'll give it my best shot.

CHAPTER ELEVEN

It's like something you'd see in an auto-repair shop, this methodic dismantling of Margaret Cooper. If you've never seen a human being reduced to his or her component parts during an autopsy, it's not a sight you'll soon forget—although you may want to.

Cooper's skin is peeled back, her bones are cracked open with a sickening pop! and her organs are weighed and commented on into a tape recorder, then bagged and tagged.

Assistant medical examiner Ulysses Keats performs Cooper's autopsy with the dispassion of a neighborhood butcher producing select cuts. As he does, the blood dribbling from Cooper's body looks more like used motor oil than a once-life-sustaining river of red.

I was able to get into the medical examiner's building because my attorney sister, Camille, is one of Dr. Keats's golf buddies, and his on-again off-again girlfriend. Also because most of the staff is off Saturdays, lowering the risk of someone challenging my presence.

Frankly, I don't know if this was such a great idea as I peek at Cooper's autopsy through my fingers. I'll definitely be having a meat-free lunch today. Vegetarianism has taken on a sudden new appeal.

"The Orioles will probably make it to the playoffs again this year," Keats says to his assistant as he casually severs Cooper's liver and plops it on a hanging scale like you see in a deli. The liver quivers briefly, then is motionless. "Until those choking dogs do their annual September swoon, that is."

"Well, maybe if that owner would stop futzing around with the team and let them play ball, they could get somewhere," the assistant says heatedly. "He wants to be like Steinbrenner so bad, it's ridiculous."

The autopsy room looks like an operating theater with large overhead lights and surgical equipment everywhere. Keats and his assistant have on powder-blue surgical scrubs, including masks, caps and shoe covers, as well as goggles and waterproof aprons. That's to guard against the threat posed by the AIDS and hepatitis B viruses.

While there's no life-and-death intensity, there's still a sense of urgency due to an ever-present backlog of bodies to be autopsied.

"You okay over there?" Keats asks, looking over his shoulder at me. "Look a little green around the gills."

"Well, I'm not exactly dying to stick around, Doc—no pun intended. Did toxicology turn up anything?"

"They haven't even really gotten started," he says, parting Cooper's flowing black hair with his fingers. Then he makes an incision behind each ear and across the base of her scalp. Never missing a beat, he smoothly pulls the front part of her scalp over her face, the back part over the nape of her neck, expertly exposing Cooper's skull. Keats picks up a high-speed, oscillating saw and starts opening her skull with it. I turn the other way.

"But their preliminary findings indicate that Margaret Cooper was drug-free—not even a trace of aspirin in her system," he says. A cold shiver goes through me. Gardner must be somewhere beyond the grave, nodding sagely. How *did* he know that?

"She must have been hitting the grape pretty hard, though," Keats continues. "Her blood alcohol level was zero point one three."

Point one percent blood alcohol is the threshold of legal intoxication in Maryland. If Margaret Cooper was at 0.13, she could have joined her little friend Debra Sutton in Paris without using a plane.

"Dr. Keats, what makes healthy thirty-six-year-olds croak for no apparent reason? With Confederate flags on their foreheads?"

"I gave allergies some thought," Keats murmurs without looking up. "But allergies usually trigger histamines, which leave all kinds of telltale signs. Our friend here may have had a stroke...I'll know soon enough."

Schluup! I turn just in time to see Keats gently coax Cooper's brain out of her skull with a gloved hand.

That does it. I head toward the double doors leading out of the autopsy room, moving double time.

"I'll call you later on today to see what you turned up," I tell Keats through clenched teeth. "Does Camille have numbers for you?"

"Yeah, she sure does, Darryl. Not going to join us for lunch?"

His response is the sound of the autopsy room door swinging on its hinges.

When I come barreling out a side door of the medical examiner's building, I immediately see the wondrous sight of warm, breathing people moving around downtown Baltimore with their skulls and scalps still intact.

Wait a minute—didn't Darcel Moore have alcohol in his system?

I could have sworn the autopsy report Gardner gave me indicated that. Digging a photocopy out of my jacket pocket, I see that Moore's blood alcohol level was 0.09, a hair from being legally blitzed.

Clutching the report in my hands, I zip up my leather jacket against a chilly, late winter wind and turn up my collar. Walking about fifty yards and turning left onto Paca Street, I head toward the front entrance of the medical examiner's building. Traffic is heavy along the three-lane, one-way thoroughfare in front of the building, surprisingly so for a Saturday morning.

Pausing before a row of four brick-and-concrete steps leading to the front entrance, I sit on the second row of steps and stare at Darcel Moore's autopsy report. He had been drinking, Margaret Cooper had been drinking. Both had gone to Northwestern High School. There's got to be a connection. But what?

I hear a car horn blaring and hear spinning tires as the light turns green and two teenage boys stage a stoplight shootout in their souped-up cars. Suddenly I'm levitating over the steps, moving skyward as the autopsy report goes flying in the opposite direction, toward the ground.

Something is yanking me up by my jacket—my feet can't even touch the ground as I kick and flail at whoever or whatever has me in its clutches.

"You never know when to stop digging, do you—DARRYL?" a deep male voice explodes in my right ear.

"FUCK YOU!" I bellow, kicking my legs like Jamal does when I lift him up. My right elbow smashes hard against something during my frenzied twisting and turning. Making a big counterclockwise twist, I bring my elbow back around again and hit whatever is behind me with such violence that an electric jolt races from my elbow into the back of my arm.

"Uuumppphhh pffffft!"

Whoever has me suspended in midair wavers momentarily, dipping his arms about half an inch before I feel myself rising, rising, rising. Then I'm airborne, flying over the sidewalk, over a parking meter, over a green Chevrolet Caprice parked beside it. I'm headed toward Paca Street and its heavy traffic.

There's no time for a prayer, or even for fear. And certainly no time for that corny stuff about seeing your life flash before your eyes.

"I wouldn't tense up if I were you," I hear Phil Gardner say nonchalantly. "Relax, because you're about to hit the ground...right NOW!"

I relax and feel pain unlike anything I've ever experienced detonate around the area of my tailbone, then I feel myself sliding on my back and I hear what sounds like a pack of wolves baying all around me, in reality screeching car tires.

I must have closed my eyes, because when I open them I see the radiator of a light pickup truck directly over my head, and can actually feel heat flowing from it.

"Oh, my God, oh, my God—are you all right? Please, God, tell me you're okay," I hear a woman's voice frantically implore. Filled with homicidal fury, I roll from under her vehicle and spring to my feet, scaring the hell out of the poor woman.

"Which way did he go?" I snarl, wild-eyed. Several fingers point south, down Paca Street, where I see a tall figure wearing light pants and a dark, hooded sweatshirt running laboriously along the sidewalk. Whoever it is has a hand to his head. Drops of fresh blood mark his trail.

I take off after whoever it is, eager to tear his head off like Ulysses Keats did to Margaret Cooper. Only I won't pull this fool's pea brain out gently.

The thought that this maniac may be armed never occurs to me. Anyway, I feel like I could take a bullet, given all the adrenaline and testosterone igniting in my system.

I'm gaining rapidly when my assailant skids to a stop beside a white Ford Taurus parked at a meter, jumps in and fires it up. He then proceeds to make a wide right turn, against the one-way traffic.

For the first time in my memory, a cop is finally in the right place at the right time: An alert female officer pulls the white Taurus over at the intersection of Pratt and Paca.

The driver is just stepping out of the car as I race to the scene snorting fire, fists clenched.

CHAPTER TWELVE

I've seen enough kudzu to last me a couple of lifetimes, the Confederate flag killer thought idly, stretching and yawning. Up the road about thirty yards was a field absolutely overrun with the stuff, as was the lot next door.

From the front porch of Cousin Trudy's yellow frame home in Stone Mountain, Georgia, a brown cottontail sniffed the area where Trudy usually planted a small garden of okra, tomatoes and string beans.

But the rounded, weathered furrows of brown earth were barren now, this being just the second week of March. That wasn't holding back the hardy kudzu, though, which was making a spectacular bid to overrun Trudy's one-and-a-half-acre spread.

Not expecting a spur-of-the-moment visit from her cousin, an apologetic Trudy had driven into Atlanta to keep a periodontist appointment. She was going in for gum-reduction surgery, which should keep her quiet on her return. Perfect.

Because this trip from Baltimore to Stone Mountain was for cooling out and recharging badly depleted batteries. You had to think to talk, and neither of those things was high on the agenda right now. Chatting about old times and long-forgotten relatives didn't hold much appeal under the best of circumstances.

What a trip! Life on the lam in Stone Mountain. Sounds like a song title, the killer mused. This little excursion should give Darryl Billups and the Baltimore cops a chance to do their little circle jerk, then come back to reality.

The reality of coming up empty-handed as the whole city of Baltimore watched them stumble and fall on their faces.

While the killer patiently hid out in Stone Mountain. Basking in the afternoon sunshine and watching rabbits frolic.

Getting time off from work had been a breeze. Not only had the boss been ultrasolicitous following the song and dance about the ailing Georgia aunt who'd passed away, but he'd made bereavement time available. So this was a paid vacation.

With time to read trashy novels and hang out and decompress. Who knows, there might even be a night or two in Savannah, depending on how things played out.

And on Monday, after Trudy was back at her insurance job in Atlanta, Jerry Springer would be on. The golden boy came on at four o'clock in the afternoon here, instead of ten in the morning like back home. So that would call for a little adjustment to the routine.

Speaking of which, Trudy didn't have a drop of alcohol in the house. Meaning an Absolut run was in the cards. After Trudy gets back from the dentist, and I've had a chance to talk to her, I'll check out Atlanta tonight and buy some vodka while I'm there, the Confederate flag killer thought, smiling.

On the front porch of Trudy's house, the sun felt so much warmer in early March than it did in Maryland. And the air had a freshness Baltimore could only dream of approximating.

It would be so nice to get back to Baltimore tanned and relaxed. Because there was still a lot of work to be done. An awful lot of work.

CHAPTER THIRTEEN

The man who tried to turn me into a hood ornament on Paca Street isn't a man at all. Instead, he's a terrified-looking teenager, a hulking black kid who looks like he could start for the Baltimore Ravens tomorrow. There doesn't look to be an ounce of fat to his bulk—this punk is buffed to the max.

Light-skinned and red-faced, he's leaning against the hood of his white Taurus, chest heaving as he pants like a winded hound. That's because he has to breathe though his mouth—his nose is flattened across his face, courtesy of yours truly. His top lip is busted up pretty good, too. His injuries are producing a steady flow of blood that drips onto the front of his brown sweatshirt and stains his cream-colored Levi's.

If he thinks he's got it bad now, in about one second he'll be able to add a broken jaw to his woes.

"Hey, *hey!*" exclaims the officer who stopped his car going the wrong way at Paca and Pratt streets, one of the busiest intersections in downtown Baltimore. She plants herself in front of me, blocking my path. "Where do you think you're going?"

"I'm going to kill that punk," I answer in a homicidal monotone. And the sad, scary fact is, I mean it. No figure of speech or hyperbole intended.

"You're not killing nobody," the little jheri-curl-wearing cop says, shoving me in the chest. But she's so small that I barely move backward, which appears to infuriate her.

"Get your ass against the hood of my car—NOW!" she says, unholstering her side arm. "Keep both hands on the hood where I can see them and spread your legs," she yells, frisking me roughly and making my head bounce against the warm hood of her squad car.

"You're making a big mistake—"

"Shaddup!" she cries in a shrill voice. "I'm about sick of you little gangbangers acting like you own this goddamn city. *You're* the one who's in trouble." Toggling the little police-radio microphone on the outside of her jacket, Jane Law calls for backup.

A gaggle of spectators materializes, apparently never having seen a black man in Baltimore City spread-eagled against a police car and being subjected to intense public humiliation.

"I'm a reporter for the *Herald*."

"Yeah—me, too!" the cop says in a mocking tone, glancing at the mostly black crowd.

"Lock him up for helping Mr. Charlie spread his lies," someone shouts, drawing titters.

"Oughta be working for the black press, anyway!" someone else sneers.

Now the cop has redirected her attention to my assailant, which is where it should have been in the first place. "Don't make me tell you to show your license and registration again," the cop says in a threatening voice. About five additional squad cars have arrived by now, further swelling Miss Thang's audience.

A well-dressed, balding white man approaches her, his brow knitted in consternation. "I saw the whole thing," he says in a heavy Yiddish accent. He points at me. "This fella here was minding his own business," the elderly man says, pivoting with a dramatic flourish toward the youth who nearly ended my life a few moments earlier. "This jackal here picked him up by the scruff of the neck and threw him onto Paca Street. I'm seventy-two and I've never seen anything like it. This city is being overrun."

Now that the voice of true authority is on the scene, that of a white male, the female cop listens attentively—*respectfully.* A lot of black folks complain about continuous disrespect from whites, which is definitely a fact of life. But on a day-to-day basis, I'm far likelier to get it from my own people, like this little black cop who's relegated me to "gangbanger" status because I'm not wearing an expensive London Fog overcoat like the white man whose every word she hangs on.

Pushing her cap back on her head, she approaches the Taurus driver, who looks dazed and could probably use some medical attention. "That true?" she asks.

His response is to flatten one of her colleagues with a vicious forearm, then take off down Pratt Street toward the Bromo Seltzer tower. Three male cops immediately peel off after him in a chase that doesn't last even half a block before one of them tackles the suspect to the sidewalk, pushes his face against the concrete and slaps a pair of handcuffs on him.

When they drag the boy back, not only are his nose and upper lip a bloody mess, but there's a gash on his chin that will definitely require stitches, if not plastic surgery. Two cops sit on the suspect—literally—before a city ambulance arrives and carts him off.

I watch this without feeling one whit of sympathy.

Instead of taking down my account, the female cop keeps talking to the white gentleman for an additional five minutes, taking notes all the while.

"Aren't you the guy at the *Herald* who brought down those neo-Nazis?" one of the male officers asks hesitantly. "Darryl Something-or-other?"

"Yeah, I'm the one. Darryl Billups."

It's VIP treatment from every cop at the scene from that point on, including Tameka Franklin, badge number 7238. A big fat official complaint will be waiting when she returns to the station house to end her shift.

The kid turned out to be Frederick Rawlings from Baltimore, an eighteen-year-old standout on Southern High School's football team. He had no arrest record and the white Taurus turned out to be his mom's.

A kid with no priors and his first brush with the law is assault, battery and attempted homicide! Because I am definitely pressing charges. But how did that punk know my name, and what, exactly, is the meaning of "you never know when to stop digging"?

Well, there's one thing I definitely know: I've had enough sleuthing for one day.

As my tailbone begins to ache dully, I know one other thing, too: I'm gonna have to start taking martial arts classes, packing heat or pushing some serious weights. Because these light, twice-a-week workouts in the gym aren't getting it—this is the last time somebody like Fred Rawlings is gonna roll up on me and live to tell about it.

When I return home, Yolanda's car is gone and our house is actually quiet for a change. Meaning I'll be able to spirit my clothes to a dumpster without explaining why my black leather jacket and copper-colored corduroys look like they've been in a shredder.

LaToya's three black cloth bags are neatly stacked near the front door, I observe with satisfaction, including a tattered copy of *High Times* magazine resting on the top bag. Good!

If all goes as planned, LaToya, and her Barbarella wardrobe, hair dyes and outrageous behavior will be cruising back to the Lone Star State on a flight out of Baltimore-Washington International Airport at three-fifteen this afternoon.

Picking up the phone, I dial the number for police headquarters. Not only do I want to check on Rawlings to see if he's gone before a magistrate, but there's the little matter of filing that complaint against little Miss Tameka.

"Baltimore City police, Sergeant Powell, may I help you?"

"Hey, Sarge, Darryl Billups."

"What's up?

"Just checking on a guy who came in about half an hour ago named Fred Rawlings."

"Hold on." I hear the sound of pages flipping; then Powell returns. "He's gone—released on his own recognizance. Left with his mother about three minutes ago, according to this log."

"How can that be—how can that be?" I splutter. "That little son of a bitch just tried to kill me. *How can he be gone already, Sarge?*"

"Hey, calm down, Darryl; don't get mad at me. I'm just the messenger—I didn't let your perp go. Says here he ain't got any priors, and you know the holding cells, and the jail, are jam-packed."

"A black man's life isn't worth a plugged nickel in this country!" I mutter, just as I hear a key jiggling in the front door.

I quietly hang up the phone and scurry toward the bedroom, coming out of my jacket and pants as quickly as I can.

"Yo, you decent, baby?" Yolanda's voice sings out.

Before I can answer, she's waltzing through the bedroom door, followed by Jamal, then LaToya. I stand there wearing a black turtleneck, drawers and socks.

"Darryl!" Yolanda says, heading directly to the bed, where I've tossed my leather jacket. "What happened!" She holds the jacket up and examines the areas where asphalt has wiped out leather.

"Looks like somebody kicked his ass, if you ask me," LaToya says, smirking as she picks up my raggedy corduroys.

"Nobody asked you," I growl.

"Go, LaToya, go," Yolanda says, shoving her sister out the door. "And take Jamal with you."

When they're gone, she pushes the bedroom door closed and locks it.

"What happened, baby?" she says, rushing over and giving me a big hug. Not feeling terribly huggable, I give her a halfhearted embrace in return, along with the skinny on what happened on Paca Street with Fred Rawlings. When I finish, Yolanda sits silently on the bed for a second, as though she's not sure my account isn't some kind of fanciful fabrication.

"Is this related to the Confederate flag killings?" she finally asks.

"Yolanda, I really don't know," I say, shrugging with irritation. "I'm as curious as you are."

"Well, why don't they ask this Rawlings guy?"

"Because they already let him out of jail."

"They did WHAT!" Yolanda comes behind me, wraps her arms around my chest and rests her head against my back. "Is there some way you can get out of this Confederate flag thing, Darryl? Why can't you go back to being an editor?"

Frankly, I hadn't even considered that option. I have this perverse streak that makes me go after things harder when I encounter resistance. Plus, I'll be damned if I'm going to be intimidated.

"Working as a journalist," I begin slowly, searching for the right words, "is what I do…if I can in some small way help bring the Confederate flag killer to justice, I feel a duty to do that."

Turning around, I see the frightened face of a beautiful young woman concerned about the man she loves. Now it's my turn to give up a bear hug.

"Yolanda, don't worry about me," I say with a laugh. "Like I told you, when the Grim Reaper comes my way, I'll probably be eighty-five and coming and going at the same time."

Boom, boom, boom! The sound of maniacal pounding on the front door echoes through the house. Slipping quickly into a pair of jeans, I walk into the living room to investigate, but LaToya is already moving to open the door, with little Jamal at her side.

A tall, dreadlocked male comes striding in as though he owns the place. "Baby, baby, baby," Mad Dawg practically sings, "you ready to make that move, kid?" Spotting me, Dawg looks instantly sheepish.

"Bro'man," he says, casually walking over and giving up some dap. "Mr. Confederate Flag himself! You knocked that story outta the park, dawg!"

"Thanks, man. What are you doing here?"

LaToya, who I'm just noticing is wearing black spandex tights and a tie-dyed T-shirt that stops at her midriff, comes over to Mad Dawg and puts her arm around his waist.

"You're back to Houston, right?" I ask slowly, finally catching on. Don't do this, Dawg. I warned you!

"Yeah, I am. But not today," LaToya says defiantly. "I'm going to stay an extra week—John invited me to stay with him for a little while."

"Wha—"

"It's all good, dawg," Mad Dawg says quickly, cutting me off. "Why don't you help me load her bags in my car?" he adds, motioning toward the door.

I look at Dawg, then at LaToya. A shiver goes through me—God, please don't let these fools reproduce. "Sure, man. Let me put on some shoes and I'll be right out."

I give Yolanda a quizzical little stare as I walk past, and she throws up her hands as if to say, "They're grown-ups. What can I do?"

When I meet Dawg outside, he's making a futile attempt to cram one of LaToya's bags into the ridiculously small trunk of his convertible sports car.

"Dawg—have you lost your mind?"

"Man, let me tell you," is all he can say, grinning excitedly. "Girlfriend can turn a brother *inside out!* Lawdy, Lawdy, Lawdy. Darryl, man, she nearly broke my back—and did you know she has a ring *down there?*"

"So you're supposed to be in love?"

"Please! I'm in love, all right—with that coodie nooch. But this time next week, she's heading back to Houston.

"Just be careful, boy."

"Man, you think you know LaToya, right?" Dawg says, suddenly serious. "Lemme show you somethin'. Looking toward the house to make sure no one is watching, he unzips one of her black overnight bags. Peering inside, I see clothing and at least five books, including *The Souls of Black Folks* by W. E. B. DuBois, *The Wedding* by Dorothy West and *Unconditional Life* by Deepak Chopra.

"LaToya?" I blurt out.

"Bro', you're too caught up in the book's cover," Mad Dawg says in a vaguely chiding way. "Yeah, LaToya is definitely freaky and wild, but there's more to her than that. To lay up in the Dawg's spot for a solid week," he says, winking, "you gotta have a little conversation about you. Did you forget who you was talkin' to?"

"You the man, Dawg," I tell him, smiling.

Dawg and LaToya borrow my black Japanese coupe, because her bags won't fit in his car, and take Jamal with them. Yolanda was hesitant to let him go, but he was so adamant about going with "Auntie LaTara," and she was so adamant about having him along, that Yolanda relented.

"Now it's time to nurse my baby back to health," Yolanda says as the three of them pull off. The regimen starts the minute we walk through the front door.

"Take your clothes off," she says in a businesslike tone.

"But—"

"Just do it! Doctor's orders."

Who am I to go against a doctor's orders? I do as I am told—eagerly.

"Go lie on the bed," the doctor says.

"What kind of doctor are you, anyway?"

"Just the kind you need, daddy," Yolanda purrs. "By the time I get finished with you, that tailbone will be the last thing on your mind."

CHAPTER FOURTEEN

The Confederate flag killer has struck again. This time in Atlanta.

"Who are you getting this stuff from, Dawg?" I ask groggily—I don't process information terribly well at 8:47 A.M. Especially on a Sunday morning, one of the few opportunities I have to catch up on lost sleep.

"Well, I can't get into that right now," Dawg says, lowering his voice conspiratorially. "Let's just say this is from a very close associate who's a reporter in Atlanta. According to her, the cops found this guy a little after midnight last night."

"And?"

"Same M.O. No forced signs of entry. It was a young doctor found in a bathtub with a decal on his head."

I'm fully awake now. Because the Confederate flag killings here made national news, this Atlanta thing could be a copycat. But I have a feeling it's my man.

"Has this hit the news down there yet?"

"Naw, the cops are keeping it quiet until they can get more details." Over the phone, I hear what sounds like a radio turned down low in the background.

"I need your friend's name, Dawg!"

"Hold on a sec." There's a brief pause; then he's back on the line.

"I had to walk this portable into the bathroom, yo," he says. "Because I couldn't let LaToya know about my Atlanta freak."

"I gathered as much, Dawg," I say, yawning. "What's her name?"

"Marilyn Mitchell. She's at 404-555-2254."

"Thanks, man. What are you doing up this early on a Sunday?"

"Hey, dawg," he says, bursting with pride, "I *never* went to sleep."

"You're a slut, man. Just a nasty male slut, plain and simple. Later. And thanks for the tip."

"Later."

I call Mitchell, who sounds distinctly irked to be sharing her information about the killing. Or maybe she's miffed at having called Dawg on a Sunday morning and finding him occupied. At any rate, she confirms what Dawg told me, with an additional detail—the Atlanta cops believe semen is in the dead doctor's bathtub!

So what do we have here, a Bubba who rapes his victims, then kills them?

I book a flight to Atlanta and call Tom Merriwether, who agrees I should be on the first thing smoking to Georgia.

Yolanda isn't thrilled about the prospect of my going to Atlanta to chase a story that may nearly have gotten me killed the previous day. Putting on a pair of dress slacks, a shirt and a tie, I quietly listen to her protests. I'm going to go anyway, so there's no sense inflaming things before I leave.

"Are you listening to me, Darryl? Can't you just let the reporters down there cover this, and use whatever information they get?"

"No, baby," I answer, looking for some toothpaste to toss into my overnight bag. "I need to go down there and do my own reporting, not depend on what someone else comes up with. This is my story, and the *Baltimore Herald*'s story. You don't just hand these things off when there are major developments."

"When are you coming back?"

"I don't know, baby," I say, hunting for some clean socks.

"Do you mind looking at me when I'm talking to you?" Yolanda says, agitated.

I stop what I'm doing. "What's wrong, Yolanda? Are you worried about me? If that's the case, save your energy, because I'll be fine. Anyway, if I were to get busted up in Atlanta, which isn't going to happen, I have the best doctor in the world to nurse me back to health!"

Yolanda's still not ready to let it go. "Don't patronize me," she says. "This is dangerous, and you know it."

I shrug. "Life is dangerous. Believe me, if I thought my personal safety would be seriously compromised, do you really think I would be flying to Atlanta this morning?"

Jamal walks in in his pajamas, rubbing his eyes.

"What's up, little man?" I greet him, tickling his stomach. But he's such a grouch when his stomach is empty that homeboy doesn't even smile.

"Breakfast," is all he says, looking gravely at his mama. "Breakfast."

"Okay, Pooh." Yolanda says, looking exasperated—with me, I'm sure. "Let's go make you some bacon and eggs."

Nearly ready to walk out the door, I fetch my black, hard plastic briefcase, which I load with two reporter's notebooks, pens, my microcassette, a small laptop computer and the police and autopsy reports on Darcel Moore and Margaret Cooper. For good measure, I grab some copies of my Confederate flag stories and stuff them in my briefcase. They'll come in handy later.

The flight to Atlanta takes off from Baltimore-Washington International at 10:30, so I need to get cracking.

"Hey, baby, I'm about to get in the wind," I shout, leaving my bags near the front door and walking back toward the kitchen. Looking pouty, Yolanda stops dealing with the five strips of bacon frying in a skillet, wipes some grease off her hands with a dishrag and comes over to me.

"When are you coming back?" Yolanda asks again, hugging me softly.

"I'm not going to tell you until you stop running around here with your lip poked out and give me a big hug."

Looking embarrassed, she locks me up in a bear hug and puts her face in front of mine. "Well? When are you coming back?"

I kiss Yolanda before I give my response, because I know she won't care for it. "Baby, I already told you I don't know when I'll be back. There's an outside chance I may be back tonight, but it'll probably be tomorrow. At the earliest."

Surprisingly, Yolanda isn't upset at all that I may have to spend the night in Atlanta. "Okay, baby. Do what you have to do. Just remember what's waiting here for you."

"I don't think you have to worry about that, Yo. As a matter of fact," I say, reaching behind me and rubbing my tailbone, "I think I need another treatment right now..."

"Well, if you don't get on that plane, you'll get all the treatments you need, plus some," Yolanda says, grinning. That's what I wanted to see, a smile before I left.

"Ta-ta, little man," I tell Jamal, who glances up scowling, outraged his breakfast is nowhere in sight.

Kneeling down, I rub his head.

"Ta-ta, Jamal."

"Ta-ta," he says grudgingly, arms crossed.

I use the hour and a half or so of flight time to Atlanta to catch up on sleep. This is the seventh straight day I've worked on *Herald* business, so it's time to start stealing little catnaps wherever possible.

When the plane touches down—hard—at Hartsfield International, it startles the crap out of me, particularly when I look on my window and see gray spray being fanned up by the plane's thrust reversers.

It's raining heavily in Atlanta. The passenger seated next to me, a black woman in her early twenties, gives a nervous-looking little smile.

Right after I enter the terminal I find a pay phone to ring up the pager number Marilyn Mitchell gave me. She returns my call in less than a minute.

"Yes? Hello?"

"Hi, Marilyn, it's Darryl. I'm at the airport."

"Okay, this is what we're going to do," she begins, causing my eyebrows to raise. I didn't know she was going to be directing my coverage in Atlanta. "We're going to meet at a diner called the Half Moon, two blocks from my paper, the *Atlanta Tattler.* Then I can tell you what I know."

Actually, we could do that over the phone. But there are advantages to sitting down with someone who knows the lay of the land and might be useful in mapping a plan of attack.

"Sounds like a winner. Does twelve forty-five sound good?"

"See you then."

Marilyn Mitchell is probably in her mid-forties, pudgy, driven and a little lacking in the social graces. She just strides into the Half Moon, tosses her raincoat across a chair and immediately launches into business. She strikes me as a capable, no-nonsense journalist.

"They found this little freak in the tub with his glasses on and an empty champagne bottle in the bathroom, on the floor," are the first words out of her mouth. She has a Southern accent that sounds like the edges may have been ground down by some time up North.

"What's the poor sucker's name?"

"Melvin Hamilton. Dr. Hamilton. Psychiatrist in private practice—was only thirty-nine when he bought it."

Why, I wonder, does this killer have a penchant for professional blacks in their thirties?

"You been to the crime scene?"

Mitchell frowns. "Oh, no," she says, making her voice sound exaggeratedly prissy, like Scarlett O'Hara. "Those big, strong Southern cops wouldn't want little ol' me to be shocked by what I might see there. And judging from the way they've already started to go ape-shit over this case," she continues, speaking normally again, "there's a good chance I won't get close to it."

"Who's the lead detective?"

Mitchell hesitates. I don't know why, since I can easily call the Atlanta police and find out.

"Detective John Freeman. Black guy who's been on the force eighteen years. He's a good egg—pretty open. One of their best."

Opening my briefcase, I give Mitchell two of my Confederate flag stories. "These might come in handy for background when you start writing. And I have the police and autopsy reports on the two victims in Baltimore. The second victim's autopsy isn't complete yet. I'll let you copy what I have, though."

We walk through the rain to the *Tattler* to copy my stuff, and I make an extra copy or two for myself. Then I head out to Peachtree Street, in search of Melvin Hamilton's apartment and Detective John Freeman.

CHAPTER FIFTEEN

Things were tumbling out of control. Horribly out of control. Staring forlornly at a half-finished plastic container of blueberry cottage cheese, the Confederate flag killer tried desperately to ignore the television set in Cousin Trudy's family room.

And silently prayed that the Atlanta Hawks game would return, knocking off the news bulletin that had come on. The one showing hordes of hyperventilating reporters standing in the rain outside the apartment of Melvin Hamilton. Where the killer had been last night.

The killings in Baltimore were part of a larger design, were the result of premeditation based on rational thought. But Melvin Hamilton? He had been nothing more than a self-impressed, slightly inebriated jerk sitting at the bar in one of Atlanta's hottest nightclubs. Throwing fifty-dollar bills around like they were pennies and talking incessantly about the most important thing in the universe, bar none. Namely, Melvin Hamilton.

Everything about his demeanor practically screamed, *Look at me, Mister Big Important Doctor!*

If anyone knows doctors aren't shit, running around acting like little gods, I do, the Confederate killer thought with a sneer. Killing Hamilton had just been something to do, something to while away the time.

And that was what was so scary. Not only was killing people becoming as easy as stepping on a roach, it was exhilarating. Which was generating a fear the Confederate flag killer had never experienced before—a fear of self.

My God—what have I become?

The excitement of watching Hamilton frantically masturbate in a vain attempt to save his life had been delicious. As if he actually believed that doing that at the request of the Confederate flag killer would bring salvation. Little exhibitionist probably wanted to do it anyway.

Well, no one said doctors were smart.

In fact, their pomposity often caused them to be nearly as stupid as lawyers.

It was time to leave Stone Mountain, to just get as far away from this place as possible. Because something down here strips away inhibitions, the Confederate flag killer thought, frowning at the chipped nail polish on her right thumb.

Because I am not going crazy. I am still under control.

I *meant* to do that last night, she told herself unconvincingly.

"Trudy! Trudy! Girl, is there any plum nail polish in this house?"

CHAPTER SIXTEEN

One reason most cops don't like reporters is because we're always asking for something, always taking. There's usually a demand on our lips, artfully couched though it may be.

So Detective John Freeman is clearly surprised when I thrust official documents about the Confederate flag killings in Baltimore into his hand immediately after our introduction. Along with photocopies of my Baltimore stories. A homicide detective encountering a reporter bearing gifts!

But I'm not finished yet.

"You may find," I say, digging through my jacket pocket, "that the flag decal on your victim upstairs matches this." And I hand Freeman one of the flag decals Gardner left me, one I've thoughtfully scribbled the manufacturer's name and address on the back of.

Freeman is so impressed that he ushers me into the foyer of Hamilton's luxury co-op building, away from the phalanx of frenetic reporters and photographers getting soaking wet as they desperately shout and scream to get Freeman's attention. They look at me quizzically as I walk in with Freeman, not sure if I'm one of them or someone else they need to start yelling questions at.

"Damn, I could barely hear myself think out there," Freeman says, tight-lipped, as he shakes the rain from his umbrella. His dark eyes are hard and suspicious as they give me a thorough once-over. With his shaved head and medium build, the detective strongly resembles Lou Gossett Jr. "There's nothing scarier than a bunch of you guys having a full-fledged feeding frenzy."

"Well, I apologize for my colleagues out there—too much caffeine," I say with genuine embarrassment, then quickly change the subject. "I hope that paperwork saves you a couple of steps."

I've already seen that Freeman, like Marilyn Mitchell, is a slam-bam type who cuts to the heart of things with a minimum of chitchat. Not surprising, given the caseload of homicides Atlanta produces.

We can forgo small talk about women, or the Atlanta Hawks, or other male stuff.

Stretching his left arm out as far as he can, Freeman studies the Confederate flag decal I've given him. He's old enough to need reading glasses, and probably too vain to wear them. Or too busy.

"It's Darryl, right? Who gave you this?"

"Detective Philip Gardner, Baltimore PD. I was working on the Baltimore flag killings with him. He was the one who alerted me that a serial killer might be at work."

"You know Phil! We used to work the northern district in Baltimore as foot patrolmen before I moved down here fifteen years ago. I haven't talked to him in ages. He did a helluva job on that NAACP thing. How is he?"

"Ummmm…I'm sorry to have to tell you this—Phil passed on a couple of days ago. He had surgery for a perforated ulcer and there were complications…"

"Whoa!" Freeman walks over to a navy blue leather sofa in the large foyer and sits down, lost in reflection. "Damn! I'll have to call his wife." And that's his last mention of Phil Gardner. The rest of his thoughts on his fallen comrade remain private.

"Sorry again," I say in a low voice. "Phil definitely wanted this Confederate flag perp. He wanted him bad. Did this one have a flag right in the middle of his forehead?"

"How did you know that?"

"Phil let me see one of the crime scenes."

Freeman hesitates, agonizing over something. "Lemme see your press pass," he says finally. I look in my wallet, forgetting I don't have a press pass, because I'm supposed to be an editor now. Fortunately, I have a couple of business cards the *Herald* printed for me.

Grasping the card between his thumb and forefinger, Freeman holds it out at arm's length. "Come on."

We walk beneath several chandeliers so massive they look like upside-down crystal trees sprouting from the ceiling. Freeman stops at the door to the elevator, and pushes the button for the fourth floor after we enter.

"The crime technicians have already picked over the place pretty good," he says, "so it can't hurt to bring you in."

Hamilton's place is huge and airy, with a study filled with bookcases directly off the front door, a huge tapestry mural lit by track lights against one wall, a gleaming white baby grand piano near one of the windows, and what appear to be marble pedestals holding busts of famous African-Americans. Everything is so neat, dusted and perfectly arranged that I know Hamilton didn't have children, but must have had a housekeeper.

"This guy was a bachelor, right?"

"Yeah, he sure was. The nest was definitely empty."

Hamilton looks like a soft little dweeb lying in the bottom of his awesome green-and-black-granite sunken tub. "Swimming pool" is more like it—it's the largest bathtub I have ever seen. Sure enough, he has on a pair of glasses, just as Marilyn Mitchell said he would—severe-looking black dealies that resemble the protective eyewear worn in labs.

Hamilton's skin is bluish-gray and is full of wrinkles from having been waterlogged.

There's still a little water in the bottom of the tub. Freeman tells me that the Atlanta cops are going to collect that water and subject it to analysis.

An open bottle of Moet champagne that's about one-third full sits near the tub. But no champagne glasses are in the bathroom, so Freeman or someone must have been swigging from the bottle.

"We're going to analyze that for saliva content, and to see if there might be a lip print on it," Freeman says, noting my interest in the bottle.

"If the pattern follows, you're going to find that this guy has a pretty high alcohol content—enough to be legally intoxicated. And you're not going to come up with a definitive cause of death."

Covering the drain is a round, silver-colored plate with several holes drilled through it. What appears to be either mucus or semen has come to rest partially on the plate and partially in the bottom of the tub. It apparently stopped just short of slithering down the drain.

"Who found Hamilton?"

"A brother who lives in Detroit and was staying here for a few days. The brother was having a little extramarital fling somewhere else in the city last night. He checks out."

"You have my card, Detective Freeman. Can you let me know as soon as the autopsy results come in, please?"

"Not a problem. You may want to call, though, and jog my memory."

"Did anybody in the co-op see anything unusual?"

Freeman sighs. "Not really. From about ten last night till two in the morning, a well-dressed white male was reported entering the building, at least three pizza delivery guys, a couple carrying groceries and several guys who had a pretty good buzz on and were on their way to a bachelor party.

"And that's only what witnesses have given to us," Freeman continues. "Who knows who came in and out of this place last night?"

"What did you get from the alarm system?"

"What do you mean?"

"I noticed the alarm when I came in," I answer, wondering if Freeman is holding back. "It appears to be the kind that's connected to a centralized security system. I'm sure it probably has a record of Hamilton's comings and goings."

Freeman already knows this—what's up with him all of a sudden?

I guess I must have turned into another of those nosy, demanding reporters. Freeman's relaxed demeanor is gone now. And his brown eyes have narrowed and are boring through me.

"We're not prepared to release that information."

"How come?"

"Okay, show-and-tell is over," he says flatly, grasping my elbow to guide me out the bathroom door. "Time to leave."

"Do you mind if I take a few more notes describing Hamilton's place?"

"Do it quickly."

Back outside, a cold, nasty drizzle is falling on the soggy, huddled media masses. They nearly stampede in their eagerness to thrust microphones and cameras into my face as I leave Hamilton's co-op building. I feel for them, because I've done this scene too many times to count. But I'm also left with a keen appreciation of why so many people outside our business hate us and what we do.

"Sorry," I say, throwing up my hands. "I'm just the maintenance man." They have no problem swallowing that one and quickly disperse, the scent of blood no longer in the water. Walking past them, I head toward the *Tattler*, where I left my overnight bag and laptop computer behind the guard's desk. And I enjoy a tremendous laugh at the expense of my colleagues.

Maintenance man, my ass! I just ate your lunches, but none of you has an inkling, because all you see is my brown skin. There have been occasions when being a black reporter has been a distinct advantage—there have been a number of times a source has been relieved not to encounter a "hard-hitting" white reporter. Allowing the easygoing, amiable little brown spider to pounce on careless flies.

"You're no maintenance man, are you?" I hear a young-sounding female voice say. I turn to see a petite black girl who appears to be nineteen and who's wearing a yellow rain slicker with the hood pulled up over her head. Her hands are jammed into her pockets.

"Not on your life, sis. Not hardly. Who are you?"

"I'm Cynthia Travers and I'm a reporter with WATL-TV, Atlanta," she says, withdrawing a warm hand from her pocket and giving me a firm shake.

I laugh, realizing Travers probably uses her youthful appearance and her blackness to ambush folks. I definitely look all of my thirty-three years, so I can't use that one.

"Who are you a reporter with?" Travers asks disarmingly. She has little-girl bangs sticking out from under her hood and a tad too much blush. Her teeth are perfectly white and beautifully aligned.

"The *Baltimore Herald*."

"Oh, so you flew down for this Confederate flag thing, right?"

"You got it. Look, good luck with your story, Cynthia. Nice meeting you."

"So what was Freeman talking about inside the building?" she asks sweetly, ignoring my comments.

"That if the Falcons don't get a decent quarterback soon, it's going to be another long year."

Travers tosses her head back and cuts loose a tinkly laugh. "Liar!"

"You doubt the veracity of a fellow journalist?" I reply, feigning indignation.

"In this case, yeah—yeah, I do. Where are you headed?"

"Well, I'm gonna get out of this drizzle, for one thing. Then I'll probably grab some dinner at some point." I fail to mention that I'm also going to try to track down Hamilton's receptionist, his brother, as well as some of his neighbors.

"Would you like some company for dinner?"

"Sure, why not?" I answer unhesitatingly. "That is, if I get a chance. I've still got to send a story to my paper for tomorrow's editions."

Travers writes her home phone number on the back of a business card.

"Where are you staying down here?"

"I made a reservation at Bertha's, a black bed-and-breakfast downtown. I haven't checked in yet, though."

"I know exactly where that is. Let's try to hook up later, okay?"

"Fine," I answer, curious why she's so interested in joining me for dinner. "See you later."

CHAPTER SEVENTEEN

Frederick Rawlings's mind was made up—to hell with the court magistrate and his order to remain in Baltimore. Given what Rawlings had done in the past twenty-four hours, what difference would it make if he disobeyed a magistrate?

The damage was already done. To his teenage way of thinking, nothing could ever erase the disgrace and shame he'd brought on his family. And himself.

Anyway, his boys—half of whom had already been through the court system—were warning that Maryland was about to start sending teenagers convicted of murder, or attempted murder, straight to the gas chamber.

Why had he attacked Darryl Billups, whom he easily recognized from numerous newspaper and television appearances? If he only knew where to find Mr. Billups, he would apologize from the heart.

The best way to deal with things was to leave, just disappear, Fred reasoned. Even if it meant giving up the family he loved, the camaraderie of his friends and the C average he'd struggled so mightily to achieve at Southern High. Even if it meant turning his back on his cherished dream of playing in the National Football League.

He would use $495.34 earned doing backbreaking labor with a landscaping company during the summer to fund his escape. Part of the stash was hidden in a dresser drawer, the other part in the closet, in his only pair of dress shoes. Size 18D.

Removing the money from its hiding places as tears streamed down his face, the panic-stricken teenager stuffed low-denomination bills and coins into the pockets of his Southern High jacket until they bulged.

When he left his room, his mother confronted him immediately about his red, puffy eyes, wanting to know if he was on drugs or something. Assuring his mother that wasn't the case, he then hugged her, an unusually long and loving embrace, his mother thought.

"You okay, Freddie?"

"Yeah, Ma. I'm just going over Junior's house, all right?"

He was the kind of boy who did exactly as he promised and really hadn't been a moment's trouble prior to yesterday. Ordinarily she wouldn't have doubted his word. Today, though, something made her hesitate.

Fred Rawlings's mother started to say something, but, given her son's already traumatized state, she elected to keep her reservations to herself.

"I don't want you driving my car until your court date, you hear?"

"Yes, Mama," he dutifully replied, the keys to the white Taurus already safely tucked in his pants pocket. Fred Rawlings numbly walked out the front door of his house, then down the block where the Taurus was parked. Calmly deactivating the burglar alarm, he drove away, leaving behind the only world he'd ever known.

Baltimore-Washington International was his destination. He'd never been there before—he'd never been on a plane or even farther from Baltimore than Virginia Beach. All that would change shortly. Fred knew the way to Interstate 95 and he'd heard the airport was somewhere off 95, so he'd find it.

The ticket agent at Baltimore-Washington International seemed mildly surprised when Fred slowly counted out ten- and five-dollar bills and quarters to pay for his ticket. Her eyes also lingered on the bloody gauze covering the twenty-one stitches in his chin, the ugly black sutures that protruded from his upper lip like cactus needles, and the clear plastic birdman mask guarding his broken nose.

But he'd produced a picture ID, his Maryland driver's license, and paid for his fare in cash. She felt sorry for him when he seemed so shocked to discover the one-way, spur-of-the-moment fare to Atlanta was $425.

"But what about them ninety-nine-dollar things they always show on TV?" Fred blurted.

"I'm sorry, young man. To get one of those, you have to buy your ticket at least two weeks in advance. And you have to stay over a Saturday night."

No question about it: Hulking, crestfallen Fred Rawlings was one passenger it wouldn't take much prodding for the ticket agent to remember in vivid detail.

When the time came for him to walk off the Jetway and actually board the plane, he paused for such a long time that a flight attendant gently joked with him, asking if he had changed his mind about the flight.

Seeing what appeared to be one very anxious first-timer, the motherly attendant took Fred under her wing, even leading him to seat 20D as he trundled down the aisle slightly bent over, to keep his head off the aircraft's ceiling.

A steady stream of foreign sensations and experiences followed: the flight attendant parading down the aisle holding a mask and plastic tube to her face, the embarrassment of not knowing how to bring his seat to a full upright position, the muffled moan of jet engines as they came to life, the queer clicking and whirring sounds from different sections of the plane as it lumbered down the taxiway.

Fred clutched his seat cushion with massive hands when the airplane finally began its takeoff run, moving slowly at first, then faster than he had ever gone in his life.

The passenger beside him, thinking that Fred was merely afraid of flying, reassuringly patted his arm just before the plane's nose lifted from the ground.

"Hey, man, everything's cool. I take this flight all the time—you'll like it."

Actually, Fred had wanted to fly his entire life—nothing had happened thus far that had frightened him. It was just that he was still a big kid in a very adult body. And he knew that what he had done yesterday, something he would give anything to undo, had permanently turned the page on his childhood.

With the enormity of his situation cascading down on him, Fred Rawlings put a muscular arm over his face and quietly began to blubber.

If there was an upside to all of this, it was that the one person who would understand why he did what he did awaited in Atlanta.

The Confederate flag killer vigorously wiggled her shoulders, making rain droplets fly from her yellow rain slicker and splatter against the beige aluminum siding of Cousin Trudy's house.

The water shimmered like fireworks in the glow of a porch light her cousin had thoughtfully turned on. Nearly vibrating with excitement, she carefully pulled back her hood and patted at her bangs, which were wet and plastered against her forehead.

She listened to the sound of water hitting the cantilevered wooden roof covering the front porch. It was just cool enough for her to see her breath, which drifted lazily toward the light and quickly evaporated.

Were the stars properly aligned or what? After she had seen the crime scene on television and impulsively driven to it, who should come striding there like the lord and master of the universe but Darryl Billups?

His stupid *Baltimore Herald* articles were what had pushed her to Stone Mountain in the first place. She had watched as he arrogantly marched up to the primary detective on the case as if no one else were covering the murder except him.

From that point on, the Confederate flag killer had just acted intuitively, following a divinely crafted script. She had asked one of the reporters on the scene for a business card, then waited in the rain with the other predators until Billups left Hamilton's co-op.

The moment he saw her girlish face, she knew she had him by the balls. He was walking a path trod by Marcel Moore and Margaret Cooper and Melvin Hamilton. Oh, yes, make that Melvin Hamilton the Third—he'd emphasized that repeatedly!

She would wear the one good dress she had carried with her to Georgia, the clingy burgundy crushed-velvet number that made her already firm breasts seem to defy gravity. The same dress Melvin Hamilton couldn't keep his eyes off, even as his silly ass was dying.

Unsnapping her raincoat, she took it off and gently swung it in a circle over her head to remove the remaining water. Like a hawk, the bone-chilling dampness was instantly upon her, sending shivers through her well-conditioned body.

The Confederate flag killer quickly opened the front door and immediately felt the welcome embrace of heat from a wood stove. Even though Trudy's house was thoroughly modern and had a central climate-control system, she had installed the stove anyway, claiming its dry heat couldn't be matched by a gas furnace. The killer was inclined to agree.

"Brenda! Girl, I just saw you on television! I didn't know you were going into the city!"

Stunned, the Confederate flag killer dropped her raincoat in the middle of Trudy's living room carpet. "Trudy, baby, you always were a kidder," she said, recovering quickly and picking up the yellow raincoat. "What are you talking about?"

"I saw you in front of the co-op where they say some kind of white maniac killed a black man and put a little Confederate flag on him. It was on the six o'clock news."

Brenda Rawlings casually draped her coat over a wooden kitchen chair and walked back into the living room. The bracing aroma of chili, especially the scent of green peppers, filled the house.

Standing directly in front of her cousin, Rawlings dug her hands into her tiny hips.

"And, pray tell, what was I doing, girl?"

"Oh, it was definitely you," Trudy replied, stubbornly pressing forward. "The same yellow raincoat and everything. They even did a close-up of your face."

"Shoot, I must have an evil twin down here, then," Rawlings said evenly, staring her cousin down. "Because that definitely wasn't me."

"Girl, she was your spitting image, then," Trudy said, uncertainty creeping into her voice. "Cute little thing with bangs—just like yours, Brenda."

"Now, you know I have better things to do with my time than stand around outside in the rain," Rawlings said, laughing easily. "Like eat some of that chili I know you made for me, Cuz. Come on, give it up!"

"You can't handle it!" Trudy teased, the co-op sighting already forgotten. "I put some of that Tabasco in there and it'll burn your little hindparts right up!"

"Well, come on, then, girl. Bring it! But I gotta eat and run, 'cause I got somewhere to go. You need to get on out of this house for a change and come with me."

"Really? What's up? Where are you going?"

"I ran into a cute little tenderoni at a club last night," Rawlings said, sneaking a glance at her cousin, who frowned disapprovingly. As expected.

A devout Baptist, Trudy had a hot date, too—with Ecclesiastes. Right on the living room couch, along with some freshly made brownies and a pot of coffee.

"No, I'd better stick close to home," Trudy said haltingly. "I still have this packing on my gums from my surgery and the roads are slick and everything...you know."

"Suit yourself. I'm gonna wash my hands. I'll be right back."

Slumping against the sink as soon as the bathroom door had closed, Brenda Rawlings turned on the faucet and exhaled deeply. Damn, I'm getting sloppy, she thought. What in the world brought on that impulsive visit to Hamilton's place?

But unless they showed her image again on the eleven o'clock news, which Rawlings doubted, Trudy probably wouldn't mention it again. Standing up straight, she admired herself in the mirror. A face that still got carded at nightclubs gazed back.

An innocent-looking, honey-colored visage that at most might belong to a twenty-two-year-old college senior, instead of someone four short years from the big Four-Oh. A face that generally snagged the attention of geriatric men, high school boys and males of all ages in between.

Just thinking of Darryl made her moist as she visualized how the night would unfold. He was mildly attractive, nothing to go crazy over. But he did have a little something about him—it was the sure way he carried himself.

Standing in front of the mirror, she decided then and there that Darryl would be the only one she would actually fuck. Then he would die.

Opening her purse, she pulled out a loaded snub-nosed .38-caliber revolver and rubbed it against her cheek, smearing her rouge. The gun felt cold, stern and unforgiving. And oh-so-powerful.

Rawlings moaned, feeling little tingly detonations starting to go off near her midsection. Darryl was going to be different all the way around—no bathtub for him. No, he would be the first to feel the wrath of her peacemaker.

A few months ago, she wouldn't have dreamed of acting like this. Or even thinking like this. She couldn't explain what had happened, but she had turned into a lioness. And whatever had brought on the transformation, she didn't regret it. Not at all.

Like those who had preceded him, Darryl would follow his dick to his doom. Same as Moore and Hamilton. And, in a manner of speaking, Cooper.

"Brenda, what you doing in there? Come on—dinner is ready."

CHAPTER EIGHTEEN

It takes all the self-control I can muster not to grab my black laptop computer, rip out its power cord and hurl it through the window of my room at Bertha's bed-and-breakfast in Atlanta. My story is written, it's 7:28 P.M. and I desperately need to transmit my piece back to the *Baltimore Herald*.

However, a demonic rectangle of plastic, silicon chips and wire has apparently deemed my effort unworthy of publication. For reasons not clear to me, because I'm not a techie—and proud of it—my computer flatly refuses to transmit through its modem and across the telephone lines.

I have always maintained that computers are like cats in that they can sense you don't like them. This aggravating episode just lends more credence to my theory.

"Little black muthafucka, you better be glad you cost four thousand dollars," I growl. "Otherwise, your ass would be grass."

What happened to the good ol' days of writing stories in shorthand, then dictating them over the phone? Which is what I'll wind up doing if I can't get this thing to work. "Bitch!"

Tap, tap, tap. Who is knocking on my door at a time like this? "YEAH!"

I yank it open and—the little girl has grown up. Damn, has Cynthia Travers grown up! What appeared to be a high school waif is very much a woman, one whose ample cleavage nearly spilleth out of a burgundy crushed-velvet dress highlighted by a string of white pearls around her neck.

And who has shapely, muscular legs with the well-defined calves of a runner or ballerina. And I have always fantasized about making love to a ballerina...Satan, get thee behind me! I really, really did not come down here looking for trouble. Which is when it usually tends to find you.

"Come on in," I tell her, hurrying back to deal with my electronic nemesis. In a second, I'll have to call the *Herald*, then they'll have to track down a computer guy. Which will waste valuable time and make me blow my deadline.

Seeing the evil look on my face, Cynthia remains in the hallway. "Is this a bad time for you? Should I come back later?" she asks sweetly. By now her perfume has entered the room and it smells exactly like she looks. Sweeeeeet.

"No, come on in," I say, grabbing her little-girl rain slicker and hanging it up. "Bear with me, because I'm trying to file my story and I'll be damned if I can figure this computer out. Have a seat."

Walking back toward a small desk where I have papers strewn all around my computer, I loosen my tie and return to my seat. Absentmindedly stroking my mustache, I read the instructions that came with my laptop.

"So who do you think did it?" Travers says, sitting on my yellowed quilted bedspread and daintily crossing those beautiful legs. Instead of tossing her purse onto the bed, she continues to grasp it tightly.

"Huh?"

"Who do you think is behind these killings?"

"Got me," I reply brusquely, continuing to fiddle with my computer. I find it odd a reporter would interrupt another reporter obviously battling deadline demons.

"Want me to take a look at that?"

"Huh?"

"Do you want me to see if I can get that thing to work?"

"Sure," I answer, shrugging. "I can't seem to outsmart it."

Cynthia Travers delicately uncrosses her legs, rises from the bed and saunters over to where I'm sitting. She brings her purse with her. "I'll bet it's a simple problem."

She makes it a point to bend over and examine the laptop in a way that leaves her healthy breasts hovering inches from my face. They're so close that I can see where she's sprinkled powder into the heavenly valley. Sucking my breath, I feel a warm flush of excitement flow through me like ocean surf creeping over the beach. Wow!

"Are you sure," Travers says, looking at me and smiling, "that the male/female connector for the modem is pressed together tight?" I don't know if that was meant to be a double entendre, but I do know my dick is beginning to strain ever so slightly against my underwear as it engorges with blood.

With women, you have to stoke the stove, load it with firewood, make sure the flue is adjusted just right. With men, just flick a switch and you've got instant heat. And Travers has me burning up. I briefly visualize the two of us naked in bed with the quilted bedsheet thrown on the floor and me grabbing her tight buns with both hands as I slide in and out...all night long. It's clear where the little head wants to go with this one.

The big one is saying something about Yolanda and Jamal and fidelity and AIDS. Damn, should I be thinking and feeling this way when I'm living with someone who has a good shot of becoming my wife?

"What did you say?" I finally reply, hooking my shirt collar with two fingers and pulling it away from my neck to let some cool air in. I back away from Travers slightly.

What's up with this woman—her picture must be in the dictionary beside "aggressive." I'm flattered by the attention, but why couldn't this have happened about a year ago, when Yolanda wasn't in the picture?

Still holding on tight to her precious purse, Travers walks over to the phone jack in the wall and gently unsnaps it. Her plum nail polish glistens as she runs her hand along the length of plastic phone line, up to where it connects with my computer. "There are a couple of connectors here," she says, frowning as she unplugs the phone line. "Did you try both?"

"Yep."

"Well, let's give this other one another shot just in case."

I try to dial through to the *Herald*'s computers again and the little laptop pops, hisses, then dutifully starts transmitting my story.

I look up gratefully and smile at Travers, who is back on the bed again with her legs crossed. There are two chairs in my room—why does she have to get on my bed? Travers is staring directly at me, but her mind appears to be elsewhere and her expression is sad, almost pained.

"What are you thinking about?"

"Oh, nothing," she replies quietly. "Just about something I have to do."

"Doesn't look as though you're looking forward to it," I say, turning my attention back to my portable computer, which happily hums as it spits out its precious cargo.

"Not at all, Darryl." Travers sighs, looking at me sadly. "I wish I didn't have to."

"Well, then," I say, laughing, "if no one is going to die as a direct result of avoiding whatever it is, why not skip it? Especially if it's making you look that sad!"

Travers averts her eyes and shifts her weight on the bed. Seeing that whatever is bothering her is rubbing a nerve, and feeling upbeat myself, I change the subject.

"You're the native around these parts—where should we go to grab something to eat?"

Travers glides off the bed again and stands directly beside me. I inhale deeply of her perfume, which must be made of ginseng, Spanish fly and every other aphrodisiac known to man, given the effect it's having on me. Still clutching her purse, she rubs her free hand across my collar and the back of my neck.

She bends over slightly, brushing one of her breasts lightly across the top of my head. I hear her dress rustle against her nylons. In a way that could only be described as nonchalant, Travers unfastens the top three buttons on my shirt, her hand slowly lingering over each button. And I don't stop her, either.

Satisfied that enough buttons are loose for her to take care of business, this smooth seductress slowly slips her hand beneath my undershirt and starts running it through the hairs on my chest. With each circular motion of her hand, a little more blood flows out of my brain.

I have no doubt she can see my erection now, nor do I care. Her every move is telling me that's exactly what she wanted to see.

"Are you *sure* you want to go out to a restaurant?" Travers's voice makes it clear that if I say yes, I'm some kind of village idiot. "We could send out for Chinese or something."

In another second or so, there will be no turning back. It takes every ounce of resolve I have to reach under my shirt, grab Travers's hand and gently remove it from my chest. I heave the deepest of sighs.

"No," I tell her in a slightly strained voice, because I feel as if I can barely breathe. "No, I am definitely not sure—not at all. Which is why we definitely need to leave my room and go somewhere else."

"That's a shame," Travers says, clearly disappointed. "Is it me?"

I laugh, then stop when I see the hurt look on her face. "You've got to be kidding. No, it definitely isn't you. I, uh, have someone back home..." I stop, searching for the proper words. Because it's not one hundred percent clear to me, either, why we're not locked in a sweaty embrace right now. That sure would have been the case a year ago.

"I'm dealing with someone I feel like I could marry. I've never felt like that about anybody before, so I don't think it would be right..." My African manroot would beg to differ. If anything, it feels like it's gotten harder since Travers stopped caressing me.

"Um, I, uh, noticed there's a restaurant about two blocks from here," Travers says, sounding embarrassed. "I've always wanted to try it. That is, if you don't mind a little stroll in the rain."

She waits patiently through about twenty-five minutes of back and forth with my temporary editors, whom I have promised to call again in another hour to check and see if they have additional questions.

The weather is absolutely miserable as Travers and I step outside to walk down the street for dinner. A near gale-force wind is blowing cold, misting rain so hard we have to lean forward just to walk. When we stop at an intersection to cross the street, the stoplights are waggling furiously, as if trying to break away from their moorings and take flight.

"Didn't you drive?" I nearly shout to be heard above the wind, which is moaning and whistling through nearby trees and phone wires. A blue plastic trash bag whips past, bouncing along like tumbleweed in an old Western.

"Yeah, I'm a couple of blocks further down," Travers yells in a voice I have to strain to hear over the maelstrom.

"Why did you park all the way down there?" I ask, furrowing my brow.

"I need the exercise," Travers says, looking away.

A chilly walk in the rain was just the tonic I needed to rescue me from the overheated state I was in at Bertha's. I'll follow up dinner with a firm handshake, then send Travers on her way, I think. My hunter-gatherer days are over.

The name of the place we come to following a punishing two-block stroll is the Prime Rib. I look around after we enter, surprised this restaurant is on Travers's list of places to visit.

What appears to be a 1700s musket graces the wall over the entranceway to the main dining area. The dull brown head of a monstrous moose, complete with huge, dust-covered antlers, graces the wall directly to the right of the entrance.

A spoked wooden wheel of the kind used to steer Revolutionary War sailing ships is hooked to another wall, opposite a huge bay window with square panes of glass that I'm surprised aren't blowing away in the storm.

There's a huge fireplace with a fire roaring in it, and over the mantel is a painting of the Battle of Bunker Hill that for some reason features about fifty British redcoats.

All the tables and chairs are made from sturdy, rustic-looking oak, and the tables are covered with a simple white tablecloth. Each table has a tiny model of a masted sailing ship as its centerpiece. Strange decor, to say the least.

We appear to be the only diners inside this wonderful, Revolutionary-era establishment this evening.

I glance quizzically at Travers out of the corner of my eye.

"So what kind of food does this place have?" I ask non-judgmentally. As long as slave masters don't start streaming out of the kitchen, looking for runaways, this place is as good as any. Because the only thing I've shoved into my face all day is a small bag of chips and a bottle of root beer.

"I hear the food is supposed to be pretty good," Travers answers quickly, almost a little defensively, as though she's as surprised by this place as I am.

A waiter who appears to have gotten lost on his way to a Paul Revere look-alike contest comes and takes our coats and seats us at a table near the fireplace.

It's damn hard to keep my eyes off Travers from the moment she removes her raincoat. I am head over heels in lust with this woman. She's attractive in a girlish kind of way, although not spectacularly so. The women who turn me on the most aren't necessarily the ones who stop men dead in their tracks, but those with an aura of mystery about them.

"They don't have laws in Georgia about having dinner with nineteen-year-olds, do they?" I ask, slyly trying to ascertain her age. My guess is twenty-eight or thereabouts.

"You're so kind," she says without a hint of a blush. "But I celebrated my thirty-sixth recently. And I've got the wrinkles to prove it."

"What wrinkles?" I kid.

"So what do you make of this Confederate flag stuff?" Travers says abruptly. "Who do you think is doing this?"

I hesitate for a second as I glance at the menu. "Some sicko, obviously. I mean, serial killers tend to be twisted sisters in the first place, right?"

Travers is silent. When I look up, she appears to be upset. A strange chick, this little Atlanta television reporter. Attractive, but strange.

"Why do you say that?" she asks intensely.

"Say what?"

"That the killer is twisted."

I lay my menu down on the table and look directly at Travers, whose lovely face reflects the flickering light from the fireplace. My stomach audibly complains about the neglect it's being subjected to.

"What do you mean, why do I say that? It's kind of evident, don't you think? I mean, society sort of frowns on people who feel like they have carte blanche to snuff out other people!"

Picking up my menu again, I look for something that won't take an eternity to prepare.

"And I tell you something else, too," I continue, trying to get Paul Revere's attention. "I don't think we're dealing with any white supremacist here, either. Ever hear of a white supremacist going into black neighborhoods on a regular basis?"

When I look up this time, Travers has a blank expression.

"You okay?"

"Oh, yes. Your theories are...interesting."

"And what about you—what do you think is going on here?"

"I don't have to think—I *know* what's going on."

"Oh, really!"

"Yep. Some redneck is killing these people, then leaving those flags behind to taunt the cops."

"And how is this disgusting piece of shit killing these people?"

"So you agree a redneck is probably behind this?" Travers asks hopefully.

"Well, redneck, Eskimo—whoever is doing this is despicable. And deserves to be shot, electrocuted and then burned in a public square, if you ask me," I add forcefully.

I'm startled when Travers bursts into loud, maniacal laughter that sets her fulsome chest quivering.

"Is that funny?"

"No," she retorts sharply. "It isn't. Not in the least. To listen to you, we should just get rid of everyone who can't play by the rules—makes no difference if they're retarded or criminally insane."

"No, I didn't say that—"

"But that *sure* is what I just heard. Let's just kill the Confederate flag killer. Regardless of who it is, and regardless of what may be wrong with him."

I hold up my hand. I'm not about to sit here and debate the merits of whether we should coddle this creep or flick the switch. Plus, I don't want to come off like some raving death-penalty advocate, which I'm not. Anyway, Travers looks to be in a feisty, argumentative mood, while I just want to enjoy a good meal, call my baby and go to bed—alone.

"Whatever. Why don't we just get the killer a condo on Hilton Head and a lifetime supply of tennis balls?"

Travers looks clearly irritated and I don't blame her.

"I apologize for that," I tell her. "Let me make it up to you by getting you the fattest, juiciest steak in da joint. It's the least I can do after you got my computer up and running."

She gives me a tight smile, suddenly quite interested in her menu.

When Paul Revere finally arrives, I order grilled fillet of beef with glazed mushrooms, carrots, broccoli, ranch fries and a Coke. And I plan on getting dessert, too. The *Herald* has gotten 150 percent from me today, so I have no trouble eating well at its expense.

Travers is content with fettuccine Alfredo, roasted plum tomatoes and a screwdriver.

"You sure you don't want anything to drink?" she asks, suddenly all warm and friendly again.

"Positive. I would just fall asleep in front of you, which would make for a boring date." I smile. "So how long have you been a reporter here and which one-stoplight towns did you pay your dues in?"

"I'm pretty new here, actually," Travers says easily. Her purse suddenly drops to the floor with a resounding thud.

"What do you have in there, a ton of bricks?" I ask, bending to retrieve it for her. She brushes my hand away and scoops it up herself.

"Just women's unmentionables," she says, smiling demurely.

Women's unmentionables? Sounds like an anvil to me, but I just leave it alone.

"Will I see your Confederate flag piece on the eleven o'clock news tonight?

Travers sighs. "I was on the air at six, but I think they're going to freshen up their report for the eleven. Where's your wedding ring, Darryl? Are you really secretly married?"

I laugh, feeling a little embarrassed. "Nooo. What about you—where's your band of gold?"

"I was married once, about ten years ago. It lasted all of fourteen months, and I never went back to the well."

"Well, you know how it goes. When you least expect it—pow!"

"Yeah...I guess."

Our food arrives and all my parents' home training goes by the wayside. I attack my plate like a ravenous dog and pray that Travers is smart enough to keep her fingers and hands clear, lest she draw back a nub.

She orders a second screwdriver and then a third. Other than making her a little giggly, the alcohol seems to have no effect on her. And she keeps trying to get me to join in, as though having dinner without alcohol is inconceivable.

By the time we finish eating dinner, I'm good and lethargic.

"It was really nice meeting you, Cynthia," I tell her at the front door of the restaurant after paying for our dinners. "Good luck with your career."

Stone-faced, Travers stares out the door at windswept mist turned fiery orange by a neon sign atop a building across the street. She opens her purse slowly and, with exaggerated deliberateness, reaches inside. Bathed in a brilliant, demonic orange glow, she stands there with her hand in her purse, feeling for something.

"I'm sorry, folks, but it's time for me to lock the door. We're closing down for the night." It's Paul Revere, who probably can't wait to shed his ridiculous get-up and put on some real clothes.

Looking supremely irritated, Travers snaps her purse shut.

"You take care," I tell her. "I need to go inside and use the phone for a quick second. Is that okay?" I ask Paul Revere, who nods. I don't really need to use the phone—I just don't want to be tempted by Travers again. It was difficult enough saying no the first time.

She walks over to me, puts her hands on my shoulders and gives me a quick peck on the lips. "I have a feeling we'll be seeing each other again," she says as if she's sure of it. Then she slowly brings her yellow hood over her head and carefully tucks in her bangs. Looking back one more time with a mysterious smile, Travers opens the door and turns left, a direction that takes her into the howling wind and away from my bed-and-breakfast.

I reenter the now darkened dining room and watch Travers to make sure she keeps going. And to make sure no one accosts her. She looks back twice, but continues to head in the direction of her car.

Only after she vanishes into the mist do I leave the Prime Rib and quickly walk to Bertha's.

CHAPTER NINETEEN

Cynthia Travers's sweet scent is still in the air when I reenter my room.

One side of me wishes the rest of her were still here, too. As the old folks say, she definitely makes my nature rise. Noticing that the bathroom light is on, I enter the bathroom and hang my overcoat over the shower, so it can drip dry.

I called the *Herald* in the middle of dinner and night editor Russell Tillman informed me that everything was okay with my story. There were a few minor questions that I answered with no problem. Now it's time for a call I've been looking forward to all day.

Flopping onto my quilt-covered bed and causing it to creak in protest, I grab the phone off the nightstand next to the bed and phone home. Yolanda answers after one ring.

"Hello?" she spits out anxiously.

"Hey, baby?"

"Darryl?"

"Nobody else better be saying hey, baby." I laugh, delighted to hear my lover's voice.

"Well, it was nice of you to finally get around to calling." The tone is sharp, on the verge of belligerent. That of a terrified parent whose missing child was found goofing off somewhere, and now is in danger of being beheaded.

"I called you from the airport as soon as I got into Atlanta. Did you check the messages?"

"No!"

"Well, then, how can you have a case of the ass with me? Does that seem logical?" Silence. I momentarily think of Travers, driving home by herself. In the rain. Probably to sleep in a cold, empty bed. And I sent her packing to deal with this?

"I'm sorry," Yolanda says finally. "I just have been worried about you all day. I just have a feeling...never mind. Do you love me, Darryl?"

"Of course, baby." This display of insecurity is something new. "Is everything okay up there, Yolanda? How's Jamal?"

"We're all fine. We miss you."

"I miss you guys, too."

"So...got your girlfriend in there with you?"

So that's what this is all about? "No, Yo, I just sent her home. Her perfume is still in the room, though."

"Darryl! That's not funny."

"Yolanda."

"Yes."

"There's no place I'd rather be right now than lying in bed with you, with your head resting on my chest. I don't want anybody else and I damn sure ain't lookin'. Got that, lady?"

A male voice comes across the line, laughing loudly at something in the background. Now it's my turn to feel a pang of insecurity.

"You've been sweating me and you've had your boyfriend there the whole time. Who's that?"

"Ol' crazy Mad Dawg and LaToya dropped by. They are in the family room watching a video. I was watching, too, until you called."

"Yolanda."

"Yes!"

"Where are you in the house?"

"I'm in the bedroom," she says, starting to giggle. "*Why*, Darryl?"

"You *know*!" I say in my best Mac Daddy voice. "Don't you feel like closing the bedroom door, lying down on the bed and talking dirty to your man?"

"Darryl! Your best friend and my sister are right in the next room! You have a one-track mind, you know that?"

"Thank you, baby. I know I'm a fiend—and proud of it."

"Ain't that the truth," Yolanda says quietly, and we both crack up.

"Sure you don't want to close the door?"

"Boy, there is no hope for you," She says in mock exasperation. "When are you coming home?"

"Unless something else happens, sometime tomorrow. Can't wait to see you."

"Me, either."

"Love ya."

"Me, too."

"Bye."

"Bye."

I continue to lie on the bed, listening to the static on the line until the dial tone abruptly kicks in. There's nothing like a shiny new love, when you can't get enough of the person around whom the sun, moon and stars suddenly revolve.

And you always hope that giddy, intoxicating feeling will last forever. But it never does.

Rolling out of bed, I put the phone receiver back on the hook and turn on the beat-up-looking black television in my room.

It's seven minutes before eleven, giving me barely enough time to wash my face, brush my teeth and floss before the news comes on. The little silver volume knob on the television comes off in my hand when I attempt to turn up the volume loud enough for me to hear in the bathroom.

I'm just beginning to floss grilled fillet of beef out of my teeth when I hear the theme music for WATL's news program, then the solemn intonations of the station's lead anchor.

"...and from the scene of what appears to be a Confederate flag killing here in Atlanta, here's Cynthia Travers."

I rush out of the bathroom in time to see a wispy blonde wearing a green trench coat as she does a stand-up report in front of Hamilton's co-op. Her eyes are nearly closed against unrelenting wind and rain, which nearly drown out her report while whipping at her microphone.

Stunned, I drop my cylindrical container of dental floss to the floor.

CHAPTER TWENTY

As she drove along Route 78, on her way back to Stone Mountain, Brenda Rawlings's thoughts were dominated by Darryl Billups. She had had every intention of sending a .38-caliber slug crashing into his head in the doorway of the Prime Rib. But she couldn't bring herself to fire the revolver she had fondled inside her black purse. She had managed to brush her fingertip across the icy steel trigger a couple of times...but that was it.

"Damn, that was sorry, Brenda," she said, shaking her head disgustedly.

It wasn't that she couldn't kill Billups—no problem there. Other than a mild sexual attraction, she felt nothing special for him.

It was just that bloodletting was so repugnant, so disgusting. It was a damned Neanderthal, brutal thing to do, something a man would stoop to in a moment of testosterone-fueled rage.

I, on the other hand, am the epitome of cool, Rawlings thought. *I am efficient and I do not inflict pain.* Not one drop of Darcel Moore's blood had been spilled, or Margaret Cooper's or Melvin Hamilton's. None of them had really suffered, and their families had an intact shell to shriek and moan and properly grieve over.

But the element of surprise had been critical to achieving those three deaths. And that was something that had been forever lost with Darryl Billups.

Out of nowhere, an overpowering urge to cry suddenly overcame Brenda Rawlings. She quickly pulled over to the shoulder of Route 78, barely able to see through the rain-splattered windshield and her brimming eyes. Activating her emergency blinkers, Rawlings cut loose one howling sob after another, crying like she had at her mother's funeral.

"What is wrong with you?" she screamed, pounding the steering wheel with her tiny fists. "You're losing it, girl—what the fuck is wrong with you?"

Impulsively yanking the snub-nosed .38 out of her purse, Rawlings held it against her right temple. Closing her eyes and taking a deep breath, she cocked the hammer with her thumb. And waited for what she imagined would be a tremendous flash of blue light, followed by nothingness. Her hand never trembled in the slightest.

She sat in that position for a good ten minutes, until the torrent of rage and self-hate billowing inside her subsided. Taking care to ease the hammer back slowly, Rawlings let the gun fall from her right hand, onto the car seat. She rolled down the passenger window and a punishing slap of wind and rain immediately leapt into the car.

Rawlings picked up the snub-nosed .38-caliber and flung it out the window. Hard. It sailed over the gray guardrail and disappeared somewhere in the darkness. With the racket the wind and rain were creating, Rawlings never heard it land.

"Can't use it anyway—why have it?" She muttered.

Wiping her eyes with the back of her hand like a little kid, she flicked off her emergency blinkers and continued toward Trudy's house.

Every light in the place seemed to be ablaze when she got there—how odd!

Rawlings hadn't finished wriggling out of her raincoat on the front porch when Trudy burst through the front door. An open Bible and a plate of brownies were on the coffee table in the living room.

"Brenda, something strange is going on," Trudy said in a tremulous voice, gripping her cousin's arm.

"What are you talking about, Trudy? What's wrong?"

"It's Gayle's son, Fred. I picked him up at the airport tonight. He flew down here from Baltimore and your sister doesn't even know he's here!"

Brenda Rawlings looked up in time to see Fred Rawlings's huge body fill the doorway.

"*Freddie!* Baby, what are you doing here—what happened?" She reached up to pick at the bandages covering her nephew's chin, but a massive hand intercepted hers.

He reached down to hug his aunt, swallowing her in his embrace. Fred Rawlings's expression conveyed a mixture of sadness and embarrassment, once he saw how frightened and concerned his aunt looked.

He glanced from his aunt to his cousin Trudy, then back to his aunt. "Auntie Brenda, can I talk to you in private for a minute?"

"No problem," Trudy interjected. "Why don't we all come in before we freeze to death out here!"

There was an awkward moment of silence as they went inside to the welcome warmth of the wood-burning stove. Making herself scarce, Trudy picked up her Bible and brownies from the table. Padding along in her slippers, she went into her bedroom and gently closed the door.

Standing in front of the television, Brenda Rawlings let out a long, slow breath. She had an uncomfortable feeling she knew what her nephew's surprise journey to Georgia involved.

"Sit down, Freddie." He obediently folded his long body into a brown leather reclining chair opposite the couch. Rawlings, who now was on the couch, patted the multi-colored cushion beside her. "No, Freddie," she said in a kind voice. "Sit right here. I want to be able to look in your face."

Fred Rawlings rose, shuffled across the living room to the couch, where he sat beside his aunt.

"Freddie, does Gayle know you're here?"

He shook his head slowly, suddenly mute.

"Come on, don't make me pull this out of you like hen's teeth. Why are you here? And stop staring a hole in the floor and look at your auntie Brenda."

"I tried to kill him," Fred Rawlings said, refusing to look up.

"Who?" Brenda Rawlings cried, roughly grasping his arm and forcing him to gaze in her direction. "Who are you talking about, Freddie?"

"The guy you said was out to hurt you," Fred Rawlings blurted haltingly. "The newspaper reporter you said you could kill. Darryl Billups."

"Jesus Christ, Fred!" Brenda Rawlings shrieked. "That was only a figure of speech. I said that I could kill him, but

I didn't say I really meant it, did I? Goddammit, look at me, Freddie. Did I?"

"But you were so upset, Auntie Brenda," Fred replied pitifully. "You was crying when you said it. I thought he was hurting you some kind of way—you said he didn't know when to stop. You're my favorite aunt and I wasn't havin' it." His tone was growing indignant, angry.

"Freddie...what did you do?"

"I tried to take care of him so he would never bother you again—"

"Freddie, tell me what you did!"

"I pushed him into traffic on Paca Street," Freddie said, his tone defiant and unrepentant now. "It was yesterday. The cops picked me up and took me to jail. I ain't going to jail, Auntie Brenda. I'm not going to let them kill me, so I came down here."

"You tried to kill Darryl Billups, Fred!" On her feet instantly, Brenda Rawlings slapped her nephew hard, raking her fingernails across the protective mask shielding his nose.

Doubling over in agony, he put his head between his legs and moaned long and loud.

Brenda Rawlings sat back down, covered her eyes with one hand and slowly shook her head. "Jesus, Jesus, JESUS, please help me!" she muttered, praying to go back in time so the revolver she had tossed away would again be in her grasp.

Because right now, she would have no problem using it.

CHAPTER TWENTY-ONE

After six futile phone calls, it's becoming obvious that if I catch Atlanta homicide detective John Freeman this morning, it won't be by phone. Either he's got his pager off, or he's ignoring it. And the throwaway call I made to his office produced just what I thought it would, namely, a voice-mail message.

Not that I thought Freeman would actually be camped at his desk at seven-thirty in the morning.

Given the magnitude of the Confederate flag case, I have a pretty good idea where Freeman is. So after I check out of my room, I plan to catch a cab over to Melvin Hamilton's co-op. If Freeman's not there, I'll just go to his office and wait.

He's got to be told about Cynthia Travers, or whatever the hell that woman's name was last night, before I leave for Baltimore.

I'm jarred from my reverie by the sound of the phone ringing on the nightstand. Picking the receiver up, I silently hold it to my ear.

"Hello!" an impatient voice spits out. It's Tom Merriwether, the *Herald*'s metro editor.

"Good morning, Tom."

"Good morning yourself, Darryl. Your coverage from Atlanta was super—we whipped the *Tribune*'s ass!"

"Thanks, Tom," I reply neutrally, wondering why he's really calling. Tom can't say the sky is blue unless he hears one of his superiors say it first, so it's clear my Atlanta work is going over well with the powers that be at the *Herald.* As long as that's the case, I'll be able to dictate to Tom what I'll be doing, rather than the other way around. But let anything go wrong, and his penchant for micromanaging will be in full effect.

"So what's the game plan for today, Darryl?"

"Tom, I think I may have—and this is a big 'may'—may have encountered the Confederate flag killer last night." I say this as casually as I can manage. I hear what sounds like Merriwether spraying his morning coffee from his mouth, then spluttering.

"A-a-are you sure? Can you prove this? Damn, we are going to cream the *Tribune*—"

"Hold on, Tom." I chuckle, despite myself. He's a perfect example of someone who "falls up" into a position that surpasses their capabilities.

"I can't prove it. But there's something else—we may be able to get a picture of the killer. The person I think may be linked to this was at the crime scene yesterday, and she may be on camera."

"*She!* Damn!" Merriwether whistles and lets out a pleased laugh, visions of Pulitzer Prizes undoubtedly dancing in his head.

"I'm going to ask the cops here to get the newspaper and television photographers at the crime scene yesterday to check their film. I think the killer may have come to my room last night. This is just a theory, Tom—that's all it is at this point. But I'm going to check it out before I leave today."

"Okay, carry on down there. Just keep me abreast of things, okay?"

"Okay, will do, Tom. Talk to you later."

As soon as I hang up the phone, it immediately rings again.

"Detective John Freeman," a stern voice says. "I went through the switchboard and they gave me this room. This Darryl Billups?"

"It sure is, and I'm glad we managed to hook up. I have a strong hunch that the killer may have come to my room last night."

"What do you mean? What's up?" Freeman says warily.

So I brief him on my strange encounter with the bogus Cynthia Travers last night. Freeman is decidedly noncommittal after hearing my story.

"So what do you make of it?" I ask.

"Sounds like you almost got an Atlanta booty call, and she decided to use an alias. It could be that simple."

"Okay, fine." Freeman's indifference surprises me. "Let's just say that's all it was, then. Why was she at the crime scene?"

"Everybody and their brother was at that crime scene, Darryl," Freeman shoots back, sounding bored and impatient. "Maybe she saw you there and got wet in the drawers for you. So?"

Freeman has clearly risen on the wrong side of the bed this morning. But I'll humor him, because I'll definitely need him once I get back to Baltimore. He's your typical territorial cop.

"Hey, boss man, all I'm trying to do is help. If your people can review videos taken of the crime scene, I'd be more than happy to look at them and ID this woman for you. Plus, her fingerprints are all over my room if you want to dust. She touched my computer and I still have the business card she gave me and wrote on."

"What the hell," Freeman says unexpectedly. "We don't have a damn thing to go on so far. Why not, it couldn't hurt. I'll send a technician by. And I'll have someone talk to the TV stations. You're gonna have to go, too, to ID this weirdo."

"No problem. Can we ask the television folks to keep a lid on this?"

"We have a pretty good relationship with them. If we ask them to sit on it, they will."

"Great. I'll sit tight and wait. Any leads or developments worth talking about?"

"No. Remember the other day when you asked about the security system at Hamilton's fancy-dancey joint? Well, they have an automated video system throughout," Freeman relates glumly. "And of the three hundred and sixty-five freakin' days out of the year, which one does this sucker pick to go on the blink?" He draws air through his teeth, sounding thoroughly disgusted. "Listen, Darryl, keep me posted on things in Baltimore. Obviously you have my number here. Nice meeting you, okay?"

"You, too, Detective Freeman. I'll be calling." Sooner than you think, good buddy.

Glancing at the door to my room, I see someone has halfway pushed a complimentary newspaper under it. I open the door to see a picture of me talking to Freeman at the crime scene on the front page of the paper. Someone has very meticulously taken a pair of scissors and snipped my head out of the picture, leaving a blank rectangle. A smaller, narrower rectangle has been cut through my crotch.

I peer down the hallway to make sure no ambush awaits, then get down on all fours over the newspaper without touching it.

I have a very, very sensitive nose, one linked to a photographic memory for smells. A couple of whiffs are usually all it takes to catalog time, place and circumstance. Yolanda is always griping about me sniffing everything I eat.

Nearly touching my nose to the paper, I instantly pick up a faint, familiar scent. One that brought a leer to my lips and made me hard as granite last night. Now, it puts trepidation in the pit of my belly. My room reeked of that very perfume before I went to sleep last night.

Whatever your name really is, you're getting careless. And that'll put you right where you belong—not somewhere I think you'll enjoy.

I'm sitting on my bed half watching a bunch of lions tear the hell out of some goofy wildebeest on the Discovery Channel when I hear a knock on the door to my room.

"Atlanta Police Department," someone yells as though I'm sitting in a steel vault, instead of behind a frail looking wooden door Jamal could probably knock down.

Removing the security chain, I peer through the peephole and see two uniformed cops in the hallway, instead of the plainclothes crime technicians I expected. As soon as the door opens they come charging into my room and halt on either side of me, like blue bookends. *What's the Keystone Cops routine all about?*

Miss Bertha, a plump, elderly black lady with stylish waves in her bluish-gray hair, follows them in. "Please, let him pay his bill first!" Miss Bertha says plaintively. "I'm on a fixed income—I need every penny I can get."

"You Darryl Billups?" one bookend says, looking like he's trying to suppress a smile.

"Yeah, that's me. Are you guys crime technicians?"

"No, we're not," he says, taking a pair of gleaming handcuffs from his belt. "But you *are* under arrest. Please stand against the far wall with your legs spread apart."

With that, he and his partner each put a hand on my arm and gently but firmly walk me over to the wall behind the television.

"Could you please let him pay his bill first?" Miss Bertha pleads again, this time a little more insistently. "Then you boys can do whatever you came here for. But I *need* my money."

"What in the hell is going on, fellas?" I look at one cop, then the other. "Is this some kind of joke?"

"No, Mr. Billups, this is definitely no joke. A young woman filed a sexual-assault charge against you. Says you assaulted her here last night."

"Sexual assault! Oh, man, I know who this is—shit! I never laid a hand on that woman, other than to shake hands!"

"Men aren't allowed to have ladies in their rooms!" Miss Bertha cries out in an admonishing tone. "Did you have someone in here last night, young man?"

"Ma'am, could you please wait in the hall?"

Shaking her head in dismay, Miss Bertha leaves the room and one of the cops shuts the door behind her.

"Please put your hands against the wall, palms out, and spread your legs. Mr. Billups, you have the right to remain silent," the cop says in a cautioning voice. "Anything you say can be used against you—"

"I know, I know," I say, cutting him off. "Man, this is bullshit! It's a damn shame anyone can make a false sexual-abuse claim, and then I'm under arrest."

Neither cop says a word as they frisk me. I'd made it thirty-three years without getting frisked, or getting anything more than a traffic ticket. Now I've been patted down on consecutive days!

The door creaks open, and I turn around to see Detective John Freeman, who's standing in the hallway. He's engaged in a discussion with a very animated Miss Bertha, who's doing most of the talking.

"Yes, ma'am, we will definitely see to it that his bill gets paid," Freeman says as he closes the door behind him, rolling his eyes. He registers no surprise at seeing me spread-eagled against the wall.

"Did you know about this stuff when I called, Detective?" I ask curtly.

"Yeah, Darryl, sure did." Freeman sounds apologetic. "Couldn't say anything about it."

"Look, I told you what happened before this even went down. There was nothing to it. It happened just like I said."

"We've still gotta take you downtown and book you and fingerprint you, Darryl. Sorry."

"Turn around," one of the cops orders. "Hold your arms out—gotta put this charm bracelet on ya."

He fastens a cold, surprisingly heavy handcuff around my right wrist. Before he can get the left one on, Freeman stops him.

"That's not necessary," the detective says quietly. "Just take him down."

Somehow, I have the presence of mind to nod gratefully to Freeman, who looks ill at ease.

When the door opens, Miss Bertha is standing there with her fat hand outstretched. Indignant as hell. If I weren't being arrested, she would probably strike me as comical. "Where is my money?" she says, her hand brushing against one of the uniformed cops as he whizzes by. "You owe me fifty-five dollars and nineteen cents! Let the boy take out a credit card and then you can be on your way."

"You're still going to dust my computer for prints, right?" I yell over my shoulder at Freeman. "That newspaper, too?"

"Yep. We'd have to do that to investigate her charges anyway."

Like I've witnessed with countless other people, one of the cops pushes my head down to keep it from hitting the top of the squad car as I get in the backseat.

Numbly gazing out the window at people walking and driving by, immersed in their daily routine, I'm relieved not to see camera crews or still photographers.

The cops take their hats off, clamber into the car and we head to Central Booking.

When I came to Atlanta, to a large degree I was merely doing my job.

But now this shit is personal. Very personal.

CHAPTER TWENTY-TWO

God, please let me talk to Mad Dawg, I think after the phone rings a third time. I've been granted one phone call at the Atlanta station house I've been taken to.

I didn't call my parents because they would just freak out, and Yolanda would ask why a woman was in my room in the first place.

I never considered calling anybody other than Dawg. A patrolman is reaching for the phone to grab it back just as Dawg picks up.

"Murdoch, *Baltimore Herald.*" He sounds so professional. And at this particular moment, so damned good.

"Dawg, I need your help." He's all business the instant he hears that. "You know I'm your boy, kid. What do you need?"

"I'm in jail, man!"

"I'll get on the case right now, Darryl, and hook you up with a lawyer. A good one, not some shyster. What else do you need—do you need me to come down there?"

"Naw, I can handle it. The main thing I need now is legal representation."

"Consider it done." He pauses before coming out with it. "What are you in for, dawg?"

"Sexual assault."

"Damn, Darryl! That's not even you. That's not even you..." His voice tapers off. "Some skeezer down there after you?"

"It gets even better than that," I tell Dawg as a cop starts reaching for the phone, signaling that my time is up. "They're grabbing the phone, man. Gotta go."

"Do you want me to let your editors know?"

I think of the two editors I work closest with, Cornelius Lawrence, a.k.a. the Clarence Thomas of Journalism, and duplicitous Tom Merriwether. "No, Dawg. But if you haven't heard from me in about four or five hours, then say something, okay?"

The receiver is taken from my hand and replaced on the cradle.

"Come, follow me," a gaunt-looking, older Hispanic cop says gruffly. He takes me to a room where I'm fingerprinted. The cop scowls after I mess up the first set of fingerprint cards. "I said *roll* your fingers," he snaps. "Don't just lay them down on the paper. Roll them left to right." He demonstrates and gives me another card.

I feel remarkably composed and calm. As the squad car was pulling up to the station house, I asked God to watch over me. My mother always says that if you ask God for something and then fret and worry about it afterward, you insult Him.

Next I'm taken to a room where they have a camera and a little rectangular, felt-covered blackboard. BILLUPS, DARRYL is spelled across the board with white plastic letters and I'm placed in front of the camera.

"Hold the board up, right under your chin, please." I stare defiantly at the camera and the flash goes off, leaving purplish dots in my field of vision.

"Who filed these charges against me?" I ask, blinking.

"You don't know?" the cop remarks sarcastically as he plucks my name from the suspect board. "Some chick who lives in Stone Mountain."

"I don't even know anybody in Stone Mountain," I reply hotly, racking my memory.

"Come on," the cop says, not the least interested in what's probably the twentieth protest of innocence he's heard in the past hour.

He leads me downstairs, to an area where rowdy voices make it sound as though a raucous party is taking place. We enter a cool section of the basement where five large holding cells are arrayed. About twelve people are distributed in them. With the exception of two scraggly-haired white guys, the only people in Atlanta who've committed crimes meriting incarceration today are black males. It smells like a locker room down here.

The scruffy-looking inhabitants of the holding cells are remarkably loud and energetic, given that it's not even noon yet. Except for a couple of men who are passed out, dead drunk and snoring like they're trying to bring down the building.

Comments are hurled in my direction left and right as I walk past the beige-painted bars to the holding cells. Is beige supposed to be one of those colors like green, in that it soothes the savage beast?

I just stare straight ahead as the cop guides me to my cell, taking pains not to zero in on any one voice because I might hear something that pisses me off. Wonder what they would think if they knew my last crime worth mentioning was stealing a Baby Ruth from Woolworth's when I was nine, earning me the butt-whipping of a lifetime.

This may not be the crowd I necessarily run with, but I don't fear a single soul here. Growing up in inner-city Baltimore and spending three years in the Army will do that for you.

Although my captor hauls around a key ring containing at least thirty keys, he manages to immediately zero in on the one that opens my cell. "Right in here," he says, looking at me through half-closed eyelids as though I'm human excrement. Just another turd flowing through the alimentary canal known as the criminal justice system.

One person is in my cell, a young brother with baggy jeans half hanging off his ass and an Erykah Badu T-shirt. He has a long, ugly scar on his cheek and glares hotly, as if I've barged unannounced into his honeymoon suite in a five-star hotel.

In the black community, a stance or a glance can speak volumes. A point that white folks will spend several minutes pontificating over is often made nonverbally, and a whole new issue will be on the table before white observers realize what has happened.

I make eye contact with my thuggish new roommate for a fleeting second, because any longer might be construed as a challenge. Even so, there's no mistaking my message: *I'm as pissed as you are to be here and I definitely ain't here for your amusement. You would do well to stay on your side of our cage and not mess with me.*

Then I sit down and patiently wait for whatever's going to happen to unfold. My new friend doesn't utter a word, nor do I. We don't have a damned thing to discuss, unless he can help spring me.

"Darryl Billups!" It's the Hispanic cop again. "We need you for a lineup."

"The woman who's accused me is going to be there, isn't she?"

"Uh-huh."

I wind up waiting around in the lineup with four other black men, when a detective abruptly enters the room. "The rest of you guys are going back to your holding cells," he says. "Darryl Billups, you're free to leave." He starts to walk out the door leading to the lineup room.

"Hey! I can walk out of here, right?"

"That's right," he says, sounding and looking peeved. "The woman who brought these charges against you said she was going to the bathroom. But she just left the building—nobody knows where she is. We checked out her address and phone number and they're both bogus. You and your girlfriend have a spat or something?"

"No, my girlfriend is in Baltimore. This woman who pressed these charges, was she kind of petite, cute with bangs? Medium brown and about five-foot-three?"

"Yep, sure was."

"Filing false reports is a crime in Georgia, right?"

"All day long."

"I'll see if I can get you a picture of this woman. Give me a few hours. In the meantime, can I use one of your phones, please?"

He points to an empty desk and walks off

I call the *Baltimore Herald*, but fail to get Mad Dawg. But I do get his voice mail and leave a message letting him know that I'm okay and am free. And that he can call off his legal eagle.

Then I page Detective John Freeman. I need him in order to get a videotape of my tormentor—who may be the Confederate flag killer.

CHAPTER TWENTY-THREE

Fred Rawlings was downright surly by the time his aunt Brenda finally returned to her car. She was being so mysterious—she just left him sitting in the vehicle, in the parking lot of the Atlanta Police Department's headquarters for two hours!

She'd never explained why she needed to come here, even though he asked twice before she left the car. Few words had passed between them since last night, when she slapped him at Cousin Trudy's house after learning he'd tried to kill Darryl Billups.

Precisely what she'd said *she* wanted to do!

She had angrily awakened him at eight-thirty in the morning, telling him there was no way he was going to miss school, and that they were driving from Atlanta to Baltimore. Today.

He'd never gotten a chance to voice an opinion, nor did it appear to matter.

Why do adults always treat teenagers like children, even though we can go off to war and die for our country? Fred wondered as Auntie Brenda got back in the car, wearing jeans, an AKA sweatshirt and a huge smile.

"Where did you go?" he demanded huffily.

"I had to say goodbye to someone," she said, still flashing a beautiful smile. That was part of the reason Fred felt so protective of her—because she was so pretty. And so small. And until last night, so nice. She was the only family member who'd come to every one of his high school football games. Even his mother hadn't done that.

Last night was the first time she'd so much as uttered a cross word.

"Is my favorite nephew hungry?" Brenda Rawlings asked brightly. "Come on, we'll stop and get you a big lunch before we hit the road," she said without waiting for an answer.

"Why did it take so long for you to say goodbye?"

"Because, Freddie, I had to wait for someone. I'm sorry, I should have come back to the car. Plus, I had to leave this person a little something to remember me by. What do you want for lunch, Freddie?"

He said nothing, still annoyed at having been made to wait so long, and still stunned that the aunt he adored had actually struck him.

"Freddie, I am sorry I hit you last night. But what you did was very, very serious. You can't go around killing people just for the hell of it," Brenda Rawlings said without a trace of irony. She leaned over and kissed her nephew on the cheek. "We still buddies?"

"Yeah," Fred Rawlings grunted, trying to sound gruff. His plan of giving his aunt the silent treatment all the way to Baltimore had just gone up in smoke, obliterated by a simple smack on the cheek.

"You know what I think I'm gonna do, Freddie? Take my nephew somewhere where they sell chocolate malted shakes and big, juicy quarter-pound cheeseburgers with Swiss cheese and diced onions."

Fred Rawlings had to smile despite himself. Auntie Brenda always kept Swiss cheese in her refrigerator so she could make his favorite meal whenever he came by her apartment.

Something was still gnawing at him, though, a topic he was reluctant to broach now that they were getting back on a good footing. But he felt he needed to ask anyway. "Auntie Brenda," Fred began hesitantly, "what about Darryl Billups?"

"Freddie, let me worry about Darryl Billups," she replied evenly. "He's my problem. Besides, I have a feeling he's going to get his," she said, suddenly laughing gleefully.

"So don't even worry your young head about it."

CHAPTER TWENTY-FOUR

"Stop it! That's the woman who was in my room!" I yell, emphatically. "*That's* her, she's the one!"

A startled video editor at WATL-TV in Atlanta freezes a sharp image of "Cynthia Travers" wearing a yellow rain slicker as she watches me and Detective John Freeman talking in front of Melvin Hamilton's co-op. There's the same overabundance of rouge, the same elfin expression, the same impression of a wholesome, attractive young woman barely into her twenties.

Most television camerapeople are male and most of them can't resist zeroing in on a pretty female face in a crowd. That tendency has saved the day.

"You sure that's her?" John Freeman asks. He and I and the video editor are sitting in a cramped, soundproof booth where reporters edit their pieces before they go on the air. The booth has a sliding glass door and plenty of people have sauntered past, but no one pays us any attention.

Anyway, WATL general manager Marcellus Tegler stands right behind us, bird-dogging our every move. He wants to make damn sure his station and the network he's affiliated with benefit from the videotape when the time is right.

"Is there some way we can make a still photo of that image?" I ask Tegler.

"Shouldn't be a problem. How many copies would you like?"

"Could we have five, please?" Freeman interjects. "Darryl, you can have a couple and I'll keep three to use down here."

"Can you take care of that for me?" Tegler asks the video editor, who removes the tape from the editing machine and disappears with it.

"Like 'em young, eh, Darryl?" Freeman says.

"Hey, when you see this woman dressed up, there's nothing young about her," I shoot back. "Not a damn thing!"

Freeman and Tegler laugh.

"So the deal is, I have to keep this under wraps, but as soon as I get a green light from you, I can run with this, right, John?" Tegler says.

"That's the deal."

The video technician returns with five color pictures of my nemesis that are somewhat grainier than the image we saw on the screen, but still sharp.

"I'm taking one of these back to headquarters to see if this is your troublemaker," Freeman says.

"What trouble?" Tegler pipes up.

"Oh, nothing," Freeman says, winking at me. "Minor stuff. You ready to get out of here?"

"Let's roll."

I thank Tegler for his help, leave the station and hop into Freeman's squad car for a quick trip back to Miss Bertha's. I like Atlanta, but am glad to be leaving this time.

"Assuming you're correct in your theory about this woman," Freeman says skeptically, keeping an eye on afternoon traffic, "how did this tiny little thing kill Melvin Hamilton?"

"If what I saw last night is any indication, this woman has no trouble wrapping men around her finger. I can see her getting him into that tub easily. But you got me when it comes to how she killed him. Your guys don't have a preliminary cause of death yet, do they?"

Freeman shakes his head and grimaces. "No," he says slowly. "So far, it's playing out just like you predicted."

"And the flag on Hamilton's head—it was just like the one I gave you the other day, right?"

"Yeah, Darryl. You're batting a thousand so far...but what about that woman who got killed in Baltimore? How do you explain that?"

"Detective Freeman, the woman I encountered last night could cast a spell over men, women, sheep, minerals—you name it—with no problem. Have your guys picked up a fingerprint yet?"

"No. You had that pegged, too."

"That's too bad, because I'm sure your police technicians got plenty of her prints from my room. What about the semen?"

"Appears to have been Hamilton's."

"Is there anything significant about this investigation that you haven't told me?" I ask Freeman, watching him closely.

"No, Darryl," he says, turning to look at me. "We've got ourselves a baffler here."

"Tell me about it."

When Freeman lets me off at Miss Bertha's place, an Atlanta police evidence van is parked out front. He glides in behind it and turns off the engine.

"You gonna be okay, Darryl? Got a ride to the airport?"

"I'm fine. But if you could keep me posted on the doings down here, I'd really appreciate it."

I open the door to get out of the car, and Freeman gets out, too.

"Just need to check on the guys in your room," he says, walking around the car to shake my hand.

"Thanks a lot," I tell him, clasping his hand with both of mine.

"For what?"

"For not letting them slap those handcuffs on me this morning, and for your help down here."

Freeman just smiles and starts walking toward the bed-and-breakfast. I follow suit, but before we can make it to the front steps, Miss Bertha is moving toward us, fear and loathing in her eyes.

"I have your money for you now, Miss—"

"Just git your ass out of here," she snarls, twisting her lips disgustedly. "Just git the hell out of here. I don't want your damn blood money."

Freeman and I look at each other, puzzled.

"A girl came by here about two hours ago," Miss Bertha says, veins popping from her forehead. "She told me what you did to her last night, you damned animal! You're not supposed to have women in your room, anyway!"

Freeman reaches into his jacket pocket and unfolds one of the pictures we just made at the television station. "This the woman, ma'am?" he asks Miss Bertha.

"Yes, yes, it is. What are you doing with her picture? Are you in on this, too?"

"No, ma'am," Freeman says, flashing his badge. "I think there's been a big mistake here. What this woman claims took place never happened."

"Well, I don't want you here anymore, and I don't want your damned money, EITHER!" She strides across the gray, wooden front porch of her establishment, darts just inside the door and returns with my black overnight bag. She tosses it in my general direction and it slides about five feet before stopping near my right foot.

A robin searching for food in an elaborate hedge surrounding Miss Bertha's place twitters its two cents' worth.

"*Hhhmmpphh!* Just go on, young man!" Miss Bertha hisses. "Don't want your money, don't want to look at you anymore. Good riddance."

I'm not going anywhere without a four-thousand-dollar laptop computer that belongs to the *Baltimore Herald.* "Ma'am, I've got to go back inside and get the rest of my stuff."

Freeman, who'd stepped into my room during my exchange with Miss Bertha, returns with bad news. "You can't have your computer," he says apologetically. "We lifted some good prints off it and we need to take it downtown for further analysis."

He hands me another of his business cards. "Tell your editors to call me."

Now I'll have to explain what this woman was doing in my room and why she was handling my computer. And, given society's view of men in general, and black men in particular, I'm sure there'll be an automatic assumption for the worse.

During the flight back to Baltimore, I briefly read an Atlanta paper to check its coverage of Melvin Hamilton's killing. Then I take out one of my pictures of "Cynthia Travers" and stare at it, memorizing her face. And I marvel at the incongruity between her pretty appearance, especially her soft-looking eyes, and her capacity for evil.

"Your special someone?" a woman seated next to me asks with a smile.

"You could definitely say that fate has brought us together."

CHAPTER TWENTY-FIVE

A red Italian convertible with WHAZZUP Maryland tags sits in front of my house when I pull up around 8 P.M., after first stopping by the *Herald* to write a story. It's dark, the streetlights are on and the air is much nippier than in Atlanta.

I am so glad to be home I could kiss the sidewalk. Practically all of the modest homes on my street have their interior lights aglow as people busily prepare dinner, watch television or get ready for bed. Wonder who else went out of town today, got charged with sexual assault, thrown in jail, exonerated and flew back with a color picture of their accuser, a potential mass murderer.

I rub my chin and needle-sharp whiskers prick the back of my hand. I never got around to shaving today!

When I walk through the front door, Jamal immediately rushes up to greet me, tearing through the house as fast as his little feet will take him. I squat down to intercept him and he runs full tilt right into my arms, bowling me over onto the floor. "Mister Darryl!" he screams with delight. That's the name his mother told him to address me by until we figure out where our relationship is going.

A big hand reaches down to pull me up, and before I know it I'm being yanked to my feet by Mad Dawg, who's hugging me with his left arm while still clasping my hand. It's an embrace brothers use all the time, rather than use both arms. It lets you show a fellow brother love and keep your macho intact.

"Man, I am *glad* to see you!" he says under his breath, beaming.

"You're the man, Dawg. Thanks."

"Ain't nothin' but a thing, Darryl," he says, continuing to hug me. "Nothin' but a thing."

"Give me some love, too!" Yolanda says, playfully pushing Mad Dawg away and giving me a big smooch on the lips. I kiss her hard and hold her extra tight, breathing deeply of her scent. This is who I should have been lusting after when that woman was in my room last night.

"Boy, you sure seem glad to be back," Yolanda says, refusing to let go of my jacket.

I steal a quick glance at Dawg and he shakes his head no. Yolanda doesn't know about my little Atlanta adventure. And I intend to keep it that way.

When LaToya gets up from the couch, I don't even recognize her. She's wearing a dark gray, pinstriped business suit, nylons and sensible low-heeled black shoes!!

All of her rings and various piercing implements have been removed—the ones I can see, anyway—and her fingernails are a shade of red commonly seen on Western, female Homo sapiens. She's every bit as beautiful as her twin.

"Well, welcome back to the human race," I tell her, getting the first jab in. I only joke around with people I like.

"Welcome back, Bob Dole," LaToya says, smiling, holding up a copy of the newspaper with my front-page story from Atlanta. "Can you autograph this for me, please?"

"Sure, after you tell me what's up with you. Going trick or treating?"

On cue, Dawg unleashes his booming laugh. Jamal keeps tugging at my hand, ready to play. Yolanda is looking at me like she wants to kick everybody out right now and steal some quality time.

"For your information," LaToya says, "I interviewed for a graphics job today with an advertising firm. Sis lent me one of her outfits."

"Thought you were going back to Houston," I say, looking at Dawg, who looks away.

"No, I may be here to stay," LaToya says, looking to Dawg for support. He grins sheepishly. "It's not like I was making a fortune at my desktop publishing business," LaToya continues. "So I may just stick around Baltimore for a while, close to my sis and my little nephew. And," she adds, "Dawg." She walks over to him and links arms. I smile, as I think to myself that the two of them seem to be moving awfully fast. I'll be pleasantly surprised if they're still an item four weeks from now.

I don't know about LaToya, but Dawg is very much a social butterfly. The lengthiest serious relationship he's been able to sustain lasted ten months. Even that short amount of time nearly drove him crazy—he was so happy to get out of that relationship, he was delirious.

"We're gonna head on back to my place," Dawg says, walking up to me and clasping my hand again. "Good to have you back, bro'."

"You have no idea, Dawg. You have no idea."

"I'm starting to wonder," Yolanda says mischievously, "if Dawg isn't happier to see you than I am."

"Don't start no stuff," Dawg says, laughing, "and there won't be none."

Yolanda and I have a quiet dinner after Dawg and LaToya leave, and after she puts Jamal to bed. Jamal may be only three, but he goes at his mother word for word when she tries to explain why it's time to visit the sandman.

I watched the two of them dying to say something, but I bit my tongue. Disciplining Jamal is a sensitive area in my relationship with Yolanda, a very, very sensitive area. Indignation and hurt feelings are all but guaranteed whenever the topic is broached.

Another area is housekeeping. When Yolanda gets the yen to roll up her sleeves and give this place a thorough once-over, she thinks the rest of the world is supposed to feel the exact same way she does.

Getting back to Jamal, personally I think it's ludicrous to explain to a three-year-old why it's time for bed. It just is—that's all a three-year-old has to know. I can't count the number of times my mother would say, "Because I said so!" if I dared to second-guess a directive. And that always ended the conversation.

I'm noticing that Jamal is starting to get away with little flippant, disrespectful stuff with Yolanda that she doesn't call him on. Things like rolling his eyes and making little noises when she's admonishing him about something. Things that would have gotten me an instantaneous butt-whipping from my father.

I got my fair share of beatings coming up, because I was a curious, hardheaded, adventuresome child. But I don't seem to have developed into an ax murderer!

Yolanda is touchy about me even talking sharply to Jamal—God forbid if I ever tried to spank his behind. But if we're going to continue living as a family, I'm going to have some say in how Jamal is raised. And that includes disciplining.

That's on my mind as Yolanda pours grape juice—my favorite nonalcoholic beverage—into two crystal champagne glasses while we prepare for dinner. Somewhere in the house she's managed to find a fat white candle that's burned down to its final inch. She lights it, places it in the middle of the worn kitchen table that came with the house and turns off most of the lights.

"I scared!" Jamal's voice pipes up in the darkness.

"Be quiet, boy," I reply with a chuckle. "I told you, I already checked this house for monsters and they're gone. Go to sleep."

He does as he's told, which is generally the case when I tell him to do something. I think that kind of annoys Yolanda, though she won't admit it.

She watches me closely as we sit down to a dinner of fried catfish, okra, corn and store-bought corn bread. Yolanda smiles and bows her head. "Bless us, oh, Lord, for these Thy gifts we're about to receive for the nourishment of our bodies, in God's name, amen."

"Amen."

Looking at each other and just feeling happy to share the other's company, we clink our champagne glasses together in a grape-juice toast.

"To us," I say, watching the flicker of candlelight in her eyes. "So how was your day?"

"It was okay, I guess," Yolanda says, cutting a piece of corn bread and delicately balancing it on the flat edge of a butter knife as she guides it to my plate. Then she cuts one for herself and butters both.

We never use margarine. My parents couldn't afford butter when I was growing up, so being able to spread it on hot toast or on biscuits was a rare treat. I swore I would never eat margarine again after I grew up.

"But..." Yolanda gazes at the candle momentarily. "I would like to take on something more challenging than being a nurse's aide. I've been thinking, baby, about going to school and getting a nursing degree."

"That makes a lot of sense to me," I tell Yolanda, fishing a bone out of my mouth. "You do a lot of the things that nurses do anyway. Have you started looking into it?"

"Uh-huh. I been down—I mean, I went down to the University of Maryland Nursing School near Greene Street and got some brochures. And I've talked to some of the nurses I work with and they all think I should go for it. I can go during the day," Yolanda adds quickly, "when Jamal is in day care, so you won't have to watch him."

"Okay. What about work—would you do this full-time?"

"No. I could work three or four days a week as a nurse's aide and go to school three days a week. But we can talk about that later. What did it feel like to fly to a different city and cover your paper's biggest story?" Yolanda beams as she awaits my answer.

I was so busy yesterday and today that I really hadn't thought about it in those terms. She's right—the *Herald* entrusted Darryl Billups to be a national correspondent and deliver the goods.

"It's hard to describe, Yo. I have worked really hard to get good at what I do. And I still feel like I have a long way to go, you know? But I'm starting to feel like maybe I'm on the right track. I guess it's like planting tomato seeds and you're out there every day watering them and fertilizing them, but for a while you don't see anything. And you start feeling a little silly lavishing all that time and attention on plain ol' dirt with nothing to show for it.

"But when the seeds come up and you actually start seeing little green tomatoes, you know it was worth it. Well, I'm seeing some big fat green tomatoes now. And it feels real good, Yolanda. Real good."

"I'm proud of you," Yolanda says, reaching for my hand. "I like to see brothers strive and succeed, but it's even better when it's a brother I'm in love with."

I impulsively make a mental note to start pricing engagement rings in the next couple of weeks.

"Jamal sure didn't feel like hittin' the sack tonight, huh?" I observe casually.

Yolanda glances up from her plate and continues eating without responding.

I lay my fork down and gently massage her neck. "You know, he shouldn't be sassing you when you tell him to do something."

Yolanda looks as if I've reached across the table and smacked her. Her bushy eyebrows slide down and I feel the muscles in her upper back tense a little.

"When did you hear Jamal sass me?" she says, trying without success to modulate her voice. The best she can do is keep it an octave higher than normal. "He didn't disobey me, Darryl. He did what I said and went to bed. Do you see him out here now?"

"Why do you get so defensive whenever I mention Jamal and his behavior? Do I look like I'm out to hurt you or Jamal?" Now my voice carries a little edge, too. It aggravates me that she *always* gets peeved whenever we discuss Jamal's upbringing. I don't recall our ever having a calm conversation about child-rearing, so what would it be like if we had children of our own?

"He's not some monster, but it seems like you always want me to crack down on him like he's one."

"Did I say he was a monster? You know that bugs the hell out of me when you put words in my mouth. Why do you do that, Yolanda?"

"What do you know about raising children, Darryl? You've lived with me and Jamal a few months, and that makes you some kind of freakin' expert or something? What the hell do you know?"

It's low-blow time now. The smart thing to do would be to shut up and wait till the storm blows over. But Yolanda and I both have wicked tempers.

"I may not be the great child-rearing expert," I snarl, "but at least I'm not beating your behinds all the time...like Jamal's father, Boone." I know I'll live to regret that one. Words are like ICBMs—once you unleash them, there's no calling them back.

Yolanda sits there, letting that one sink in. It hit hard and deep, I know. She slowly puts a half-eaten piece of corn bread back on her plate. I don't have much of an appetite now, either.

"That was *really* fucked up, Darryl," she says quietly. I would rather that she scream her head off, because Yolanda worries me when her voice gets low and hushed. I always expect *The Exorcist* theme to start playing.

She gets up from the table and shovels the contents of her plate into the garbage, making a unnerving *screech!* each time her fork rakes against the plate. Finished, she stalks out of the kitchen into our bedroom and daintily shuts the door. Shit!

I pick halfheartedly at the rest of my dinner, read a little, pay some bills. Then the moment of truth I dread arrives: time to go to bed.

My mother always says never go to bed mad in a marriage, but I'll be damned if I'm going to apologize first. Not tonight. Jamal is a good kid, but he's not perfect. Everything he does isn't wonderful and magnificent and he doesn't walk on water.

Getting on my knees before I hop into the sack, I thank God for looking over me in Atlanta and for keeping my family and friends safe. Then I climb into bed, wriggling atop the frosty sheets in search of a comfortable position.

The Ice Princess has her back turned to me and is so far on her side of the bed she's nearly on the floor. In no way does she acknowledge my existence, and I return the favor.

How wonderful to bunk down with an iceberg that makes the one the *Titanic* struck seem like an ice cube

CHAPTER TWENTY-SIX

It's a tremendous feeling to wake up in the morning excited about going to work. A big story will do that for you.

Stretching, I open my eyes and note that half the bed is vacant. Yolanda has neatly replaced and smoothed out the brown blanket on her side, meaning I must have been sleeping soundly not to have heard her. Also meaning she must still be mad. If she had kissed me on the way out, like she usually does, it would have awakened me.

My digital alarm clock reads 8:23, so Yolanda has already dropped Jamal off at day care and is hard at work at Ida B. Wells Hospital. Swinging my legs over the side of the bed, I feel nothing but regret over our little tiff last night. Why does every Jamal discussion have to escalate to World War III?

When my bare feet brush against the wooden floor, the chill emanating from the floorboards and the eddies of cold air swirling around my ankles are an unwelcome shock. With this rental house, you know instantly what kind of day it is outside, from a temperature standpoint.

Half tiptoeing to keep my feet off the floor as much as possible, I lift the window shade and sure enough, flurries are lazily falling to earth. And it's cold enough that they aren't melting.

Wonder if it's snowing where the Confederate flag killer is.

Shaving and showering quickly because the bathroom is cold, too, I dig a snazzy double-breasted dark blue suit with pinstripes out of the closet. I don't care what LaToya says—I definitely ain't no Bob Dole today.

I'll make it a point to look up Detective Scott Donatelli so we can get our heads together on this "Cynthia Travers" character. And I'll stop by a florist and get a little bouquet for Yolanda. But I swear this is the last time I'm going to make the first move to smooth things over after one of our disagreements.

I may feel different later, but right now, I say we can either make this a two-way street or else shut the sucker down.

CHAPTER TWENTY-SEVEN

Sprawled across the couch in her sister's South Baltimore row house, Brenda Rawlings watched snow flurries skittering past a window. She groaned. Snow had ceased to be fun since she was ten years old—now it was just a big white pain in the ass.

I should be in Stone Mountain, watching Peter Cottontail and friends. She yanked her blanket over her head, but the aromas that wafted to her nose quickly made her think better of it.

"You need a bath, Brenda—eeewww!" she said, wrinkling her nose in disgust. There hadn't been an opportunity to bathe yesterday, not with having to drive back from Georgia most of last night. And there had been a bad traffic accident outside Richmond that added two hours to an already tedious journey.

Freddie had done most of the driving near Richmond—there was only so much damage he could do standing still or creeping along at five miles an hour. His aunt had reclined the passenger seat and slept fitfully. She dreamed at least twice of standing in the doorway of the Prime Rib facing Darryl Billups, his face lit orange from the neon building sign. In her dream she pulled the trigger of her handgun over and over and over, only to have the chuckling bullets remain in their chambers.

It was as if her subconscious were taunting her about being inept, inadequate. Aside from being a high school cheerleader, Brenda Rawlings had never really distinguished herself much in life—academics, relationships, you name it. And here she was, flubbing it again.

Even now, beyond wanting to be in Stone Mountain, she had no game plan, no burning ambition she would gladly sacrifice everything for. A lot of people have five-year plans. "Hell, I don't have a five-day plan," Rawlings said disapprovingly.

Her few close friends would be amazed if they could see what a fiasco her existence was. They tended to fixate on her vivacious personality and attractive appearance and automatically assumed she had it made in the shade.

What a mess my life is, what a total, fucked-up mess.

Brenda Rawlings wished things were different, but she wasn't throwing some twenty-four-hour pity party, either. She placed the blame for her shortcomings and lack of accomplishment right where it belonged—namely, on her small shoulders.

Which made it all the more painful.

Well, at least the ledger would show that she'd done the right thing by Freddie, by making him come back to Baltimore and face the music. He had to deal with the consequences of his actions and he also had to get his behind back in the classroom. Because Lord knows the boy lacked the intellectual horsepower to fend for himself without a diploma.

Somewhere during the course of that wretched ten-hour car ride from Georgia, mixed in with nasty fast-food burritos slathered in hot sauce, and squatting over dirty toilets a dog wouldn't pee in, Brenda Rawlings had made a resolution not to kill anymore.

But lying on the couch at her sister's, where she'd crashed after delivering Freddie, Rawlings could feel those little cravings stirring again. And she knew they would eventually grow stronger and more insistent, until gradually they took over.

Then the demons would calmly direct her every move, ensuring that Darcel Moore, Margaret Cooper and Melvin Hamilton would have some company. Brenda Rawlings also knew she would willingly, eagerly, let herself be used as a conduit again, enabling her to taste the indescribable power it brought.

Right now, though, there were matters of the flesh to tend to. She hadn't had a man in weeks. She had tried to put a hurting on Darryl Billups—figuratively and literally—but couldn't pull the trigger all the way around.

Touching herself in a secret place, Brenda Rawlings smiled. She knew where to find a stand-in, but first she would have to lock up her sister's house, drive home and get reacquainted with some soap and water.

And a big glass full of orange juice and vodka, filled to about half an inch from the top.

CHAPTER TWENTY-EIGHT

All of a sudden, Detective Scott Donatelli has all the time in the world for me. With his toothpick twirling at the usual 33 $^{1}/_{3}$ rpm, Donatelli actually finds me a chair and drags it in front of his desk.

He's a regular Sebastian Cabot today, asking if I'd like some coffee, inquiring about my health.

"I've been meaning to ask you, Darryl," he says, pulling his chair from behind his desk and straddling it, "who wrote that obituary on my partner, Phil Gardner?"

"I did. I wanted to make sure Phil got a proper send-off, because he was a good man."

"You're right about that," Donatelli says, taking a plastic-and-metal device out of his desk that people use to strengthen their grip. Never removing his eyes from my face, Donatelli starts doing slow repetitions, squeezing and releasing, squeezing and releasing.

"I cried when I read that obituary," he blurts out, glancing around the homicide office to see if anyone heard him. "I don't agree with a lot of stuff you reporters do, but you did my partner justice. Thanks."

"He deserved it. Phil's funeral is tomorrow, right?"

Donatelli stops exercising his hand and stares at the floor. "Yeah."

"You guys gonna have someone watching the crowd in case the Confederate flag killer shows?"

Donatelli looks up suddenly. "Yep."

"Well, you may want to watch for this face." I pull a folded picture of "Cynthia Travers" from my jacket pocket. With a flourish I slowly unfold it, smooth it out and place it in front of Donatelli.

"Who's this?"

"It *may* be the Confederate flag killer." I relate what happened in Atlanta and Donatelli registers no reaction. Homicide detectives must stand in front of mirrors perfecting their poker faces, because Phil Gardner had been a master, too.

"I'll make copies and circulate it around," is all Donatelli has to say, to my disappointment.

"So what do you think?"

"You mean, is my gut reaction that this is the person who's killed three people, two of them grown men? Anybody's capable of murder, Darryl. Anybody." He chuckles and shifts his toothpick to the corner of his mouth. "But what I really think is this little doll baby here tried to give you some poontang and you were so intent on playing detective that you blew it."

He laughs out loud.

"If you had been there," I say a little defensively, "you would understand. There was a coldness in this woman that I could feel." It hacks me off that Donatelli isn't taking me seriously.

"I can be cold, Darryl," Donatelli says, leaning forward. "And I'm sure you can, too. But in the universe I work in, it takes a little more than that to make someone a suspect. Unlike the media, we don't indict and convict based on hunches, or on the flimsiest evidence."

It dawns on me that Donatelli may be jealous of my role in helping to apprehend the men who had tried to blow up the NAACP. That's the only way I can explain the verbal jabs he zings out of the blue.

"While you were running around Atlanta being virtuous," he continues, trying to suppress a smile, "we were doing a little work around here." Opening his desk drawer, he takes out three sheets of paper held together by a paper clip. Rather than slide the papers across his desk, he patiently holds them in his outstretched hand, waiting for me to grab them.

"We did a spectrographic analysis of the two flag decals associated with the murders here," Donatelli says, his tone suddenly that of a criminology professor. "Or, more accurately, the FBI lab analyzed microscopic particles found on both. They did a rush job for us, because the Justice Department is ready to press federal civil-rights-violation charges against whoever this guy is."

He pauses to make sure I'm following.

"They found a couple of things linking these crimes together—particles of latex that were consistent with one another, as well as some kind of medication called Trac Tabs. The generic name is belladonna. Familiar with it?"

"Can't say as I am, Scott."

"Well, digestive-tract doctors known as gastroenterologists use it to cut down on bowel function for people with"—Donatelli glances at some notes—"something called irritable bowel syndrome." Justifiably proud of his police work, Donatelli pokes out his chest a bit.

"Did Moore, Cooper and Hamilton have stomach problems?"

"Dunno. We're checking into it." Donatelli pauses. "You need to know, Darryl, that for our purposes, we're not linking what happened in Atlanta to the deaths here."

"Are they looking to analyze the flag in their case?"

"Even as we speak."

I'd love to know what's brought on this new spirit of cooperation from Donatelli, but don't dare examine a gift horse too closely.

"Anything indicating Moore or Cooper had this belladonna stuff in them? And can it make you croak with no apparent cause of death?"

"The medical examiner hasn't turned up a thing showing prescription or illegal drugs in either of the victims. Even if they were given belladonna, our medical expert says about the worst side effect is a dry mouth, increased heartbeat or trouble urinating."

"So someone with access to latex gloves and belladonna is linked to Moore and Cooper. That should narrow the list down pretty dramatically, right?"

Donatelli frowns and shakes his head. "That's what we thought, too. But there are at least twenty-one stomach specialists in the Baltimore metropolitan area. Not to mention one hundred thirty-seven pharmacists with access to belladonna—"

"And latex gloves."

"Right."

Frowning, I think of all the doctors' offices and chain pharmacies I have to go trudging through in search of Cynthia Travers.

"Do you have a list of all these places?"

Sucking loudly on his toothpick, Donatelli opens his desk drawer again and takes out several more sheets of paper. This time, he just drops the papers on his desk and nods toward them.

Scooping them up, I see names, addresses and phone numbers for each doctor and pharmacy. For the police to accumulate that much information so quickly, they must be throwing a lot of resources behind the Confederate flag cases.

"Are you going to circulate this woman's picture at all these places?"

The youthful detective emphatically shakes his head no. "Do you realize what an ass I'd look like if that turned out to be a wild-goose chase?"

"Do you realize what a genius you'd look like if it turned out to be her?"

Donatelli smiles and starts stroking his goatee.

"So what's your next step?" I ask him, wanting to see how far his new "warm and friendly" phase goes.

"Well, instead of running down every office on that list like *an amateur*, I'm going to see which of our victims had stomach problems. My guess is—and that's all it is—that we'll find a doctor who had a disagreement with these people."

He pushes back his chair and stands up, which I'm starting to see is how he ends our conversations.

"You may be wondering how come I gave you that stuff," he says in a voice suddenly soft and distant. "It's my way of saying thank you for my partner. I know he would have appreciated your obituary."

I spontaneously stick out my hand to Donatelli, who tentatively shakes it, looking puzzled. "Scott," I tell him, still grasping his hand, "I'm not out to do any hatchet jobs and

I'm not out to burn anybody. Thanks for the info—I really appreciate it."

Donatelli gives me a tight-lipped smile and says nothing.

An arresting black woman is talking to Tom Merriwether when I sit down at my desk at the *Baltimore Herald.* A solidly built sistah wearing a subdued, expensive-looking brown business suit and a tan-and-black scarf. It's a sad commentary on my business that an unfamiliar black face in the newsroom is still noteworthy. There are black folks aplenty toiling in the mailroom, building maintenance and security, but on the editorial side we're about as common as poinsettias blooming in June.

There are two exceptional things about this woman. The first is that she's tall enough to look down on Tom, who's five-foot-nine. The second is this woman's body language—no hat-in-hand job-applicant stance here. From the way she's casually holding Merriwether's gaze and laughing easily as they stand chatting in the newsroom, she appears confident and comfortable wielding power. The way some people carry themselves practically shouts they're to be taken seriously. She's one of them.

And I notice that Merriwether deferentially hangs on her every word and gives a phony little smile every fifteen seconds. He doesn't have much regard for anyone not white and male, so my curiosity is really piqued as I sit down to my computer and log on.

Four e-mails from black reporters await, each inquiring about the mystery lady. I message back that I'm baffled, too, then dial the pager number for homicide detective John Freeman in Atlanta.

I sure hope Atlanta's finest get my computer back soon, because I'm not relishing the prospect of explaining why I returned without it.

"Who is *that* woman? Daaaaaaamn!" It's Mad Dawg, who's just strolled over from Sports and nonchalantly parks his buns on my desk like he owns it.

"I need to work, Dawg. But to answer your question, I don't have a clue—I was hoping you did."

Whoever she is, the woman has stepped inside the glass-walled office of managing editor Walter Watkins, along with Merriwether and publisher Francis Birch. They're all sitting around in Watkins's fishbowl, smiling and chatting like old friends!

"Man, did you check out the gams on her?" Mad Dawg says admiringly. "Sister's definitely got a rack that's stacked."

Doesn't he know any better than to talk out loud like that in this politically correct age? I roll my eyes. This is the same person who was lecturing me about judging a book by its cover when it came to LaToya.

"Is that all you see, man? There's a strange black woman in here hobnobbing with the paper's top brass, and all you notice are her legs?"

Dawg starts yukking it up, causing several fair-haired reporters to swivel their heads in our direction. "No, as a matter of fact, that's not all I noticed. She's got a slammin' caboose, too!"

My phone rings, sparing me from further inane conversation with this fool.

"*Baltimore Herald*, Darryl Billups here."

"Hey, Darryl, Freeman from Atlanta. Can't stay on long—what's up?"

"That's what I called to ask you. Any developments?"

"Yeah. For one thing, that picture we got from WATL was the same person who filed those charges against you, then disappeared. Haven't heard back from Toxicology on Melvin Hamilton. Right now, we're stumped."

"Did you know the cops up here have evidence that appears to link the two murders?"

"What's that?"

Surprised no one from Baltimore has called, I tell Freeman about the latex and belladonna.

"One final thing—how soon can I get back my computer? I kind of need it."

"'Fraid it won't be anytime soon, sorry to say," Freeman says. "We're gonna need to keep it in the evidence room just in case your little cutie pie is who you think she is."

Uh-oh. "Thanks, John. I'll let you know if I hear anything else on this end."

"Ditto."

When I turn around, Mad Dawg is still loitering near my desk. "What's up, brotherman? No work to do?"

"I'll bet they're about to hire a new black reporter," Dawg says, nodding toward our mystery lady, who's gotten up from Watkins's couch and is looking at a plaque he's proudly displaying.

"Let's go downstairs to the cafeteria and get some coffee," Dawg suggests, looking at me and smiling. He wants to continue our conversation about the woman in Watkins's office. I, on the other hand, have a ton of work to do.

"No, Dawg. Busy as hell."

"Come on!"

"Already had my one cup of coffee this morning."

"I'll buy you a soda, then."

Sighing, I get up and follow Dawg toward the elevator. He can be a real pest sometimes.

"Tell me you didn't notice that body." He grins as soon as the elevator door closes. He pushes the button for the second floor.

"I didn't notice her body."

"Like hell you didn't. Like hell!"

I don't answer, wondering why Baltimore's and Atlanta's police departments aren't communicating with each other. You'd think the phone lines would be burning up.

When we enter the cafeteria, an ant is crawling around near the salad bar. That fact, along with the horrible-tasting food served here, gives me yet another reason to avoid the place. No one is in the cafeteria except for us and a cashier, which Dawg takes as his cue to start barking again. "I could work with a mature-looking woman like that," he says in a booming voice as he pours coffee into a Baltimore Ravens mug. "Yes, indeed, I could *definitely* work with that."

To my horror, I see the woman he's talking about stroll into the cafeteria. Coughing loudly to get his attention, I start waggling my eyebrows so he'll shut up.

"Oh, yeah, that brown suit she had on was on time, too. Of course, when she finds out I work here, it's all over, bro'. She'll *pay them,* just to be close to me." She's dangerously close to us now, the long legs that Dawg loves so much taking her closer with each stride.

"Aheeeeem, harrummph—hack, hack!"

"Man, you need to do something with that cold," Dawg says solicitously. "Anyway, like I was saying, that brown skirt looked like it was molded to that onion. And that's just how I would peel it, one layer at a time."

Dawg, please, please, *please* shut up. She is almost close enough to reach out and touch you.

"Yessss, Lawd, that's my favorite color now—brown. The same brown as that brown skirt. Do you hear me, bro?"

"Hi," I say, sticking my hand out as my face burns with embarrassment. "My name is Darryl Billups and I'm a reporter here. I couldn't help but notice you in the newsroom—are you interviewing for a job here?" Dawg looks like a Mack truck just hit him. I tried to get him to put a sock in it—in the newsroom and down here, too.

"It is very nice to meet you," she says pleasantly, if a touch formally. I'm five-foot-ten and she's eye level with me. Turns out her name is Florence Newsome. She gives me one of those handshakes given by women who aren't thrilled to suddenly find themselves being gripped by a man's paw. Not exactly dainty, but not quite a bone-crusher, either.

Speaking of paws, Dawg has yet to turn around. When he does, though, he smoothly makes her acquaintance as if there were no way he could have been standing there a second earlier, dissecting her anatomy.

I'm guessing she's in her late forties. Under one arm she carries a bulging stack of human resource folders and manuals.

"So, um, are you going to be joining us here as a reporter?"

She gives a little laugh, apparently finding that question amusing. "No, Darryl, those days are behind me. Actually, I'm going to be replacing Walter Watkins as the *Herald*'s managing editor."

"Oh, that is, uh, wow...fantastic. Congratulations." If I click my heels together fast three times, maybe I can disappear.

Dawg, whose legendary glibness has deserted him, mumbles something about being honored and thrilled, or something.

He and I must be quite a sight, with size 14 and 10 shoes stuck in our mouths, respectively.

At this point, I hope the ant crawling on the floor near the salad bar doesn't step on me on my way out.

CHAPTER TWENTY-NINE

Not much was going right for Fred Rawlings his first day back at Southern High School. Still a little fatigued following the long ride the night before, he took a math test he was pretty sure he'd flunked.

The prettiest cheerleader in the school, Chante Bates, shot down his bid to escort her to the junior prom. She made it seem as though being a star on Southern's football team didn't amount to a hill of beans.

Everyone was laughing at the bandage on his chin and the protective mask over his broken nose. Fred made up some lie about breaking it during a pickup basketball game at a rec center near his house. That hadn't prevented him from being dubbed the Birdman of Alcatraz. Everywhere he went, his arrival was heralded by loud, obnoxious cawing, like a crow's.

By the time the novelty of his dressings was starting to wear off, he was seated in Miss Quinn's boring social studies class. Listening to some stuff about a judicial branch, a legislative branch and a branch for executives, or something.

The next thing he recalled was the sound of Miss Quinn's shrill voice as she castigated him for having fallen asleep in class. She used up the remainder of the period ridiculing him in front of his classmates.

After leaving social studies, Rawlings went to his hall locker and discovered that someone had stolen his school ring, along with a portable CD player that didn't even belong to him.

Minutes turned into hours as Rawlings waited for his miserable school day to end.

As soon as the final bell tolled, Fred Rawlings's long legs were pumping furiously, carrying him through the hallway and out the front door.

Only then did he see something capable of bringing a smile to his bandaged face. On the sidewalk, standing near her car with her hands jammed into the pockets of a red parka, was Aunt Brenda. Looking up at him and smiling approvingly.

The entire time they had ridden from Georgia, their exchanges had been sporadic and exceedingly brief. As in, "You hungry? We need gas. Where's the exit?" Taking into account her prickly, taciturn demeanor, along with the fact that she'd slapped him silly at Cousin Trudy's, Fred Rawlings was certain he'd fallen into disfavor with his aunt.

He didn't know anyone as attractive or capable as she was. He'd had a crush on her since he was four and would do anything for his aunt Brenda—Darryl Billups could attest to that.

"How's my favorite nephew—and why aren't you wearing a hat, boy?" she said, reaching up and affectionately rubbing Fred Rawlings's bare head.

"Terrible, Auntie Brenda. Terrible. I wish we was still in Georgia. Ain't nothin' gone right today," he grumbled, feeling sorry for himself.

"It can't be that bad, Freddie. What happened?"

Of all the day's trials and tribulations, being rejected by Chante Bates stung the most. So that was the one he related to his aunt.

"Well, let me tell you something, handsome Fred Rawlings. If that girl doesn't have enough sense to go out with you, that's her loss. Because you are one fiiiine young brother."

Fred Rawlings beamed.

"How about if Aunt Brenda made one of those cheeseburgers you love so much? With an extra slice of Swiss. Would that make you feel better?"

"Yeah," he said shyly. "I'd like that."

During the drive to her apartment, Brenda Rawlings talked to her nephew like they always had in the past. She asked how his schoolwork was coming along and stressed how important it was to keep his grades up.

They discussed his work plans for the summer and which college he wanted to attend, if any. She even lovingly nagged her nephew about keeping the dressing on his wound clean so he wouldn't get an infection.

It was just like old times, Fred Rawlings thought, ecstatic their relationship appeared to be on the rebound.

When they got to her apartment, he quickly devoured two cheeseburgers and three glasses of chocolate milk as his aunt sat across the kitchen table from him, smiling and sipping a tall glass of orange juice she'd added some vodka to.

A puzzled expression slowly drifted across Fred Rawlings's face. "Ain't you gotta go to work today, Aunt Brenda?"

"You mean," she chided him, "don't you have to go to work today, Aunt Brenda? Well, to answer your question—no, I don't. Aunt Brenda is on vacation." She almost told him she was on bereavement leave, a Pandora's box there was no reason to open.

"Did that food fill you up, Freddie?" she asked, changing the subject. "Do you want another cheeseburger?"

Even though he was still hungry, Fred Rawlings politely declined. Self-conscious about the amount of food it took to keep his six-foot-five frame operating, he didn't want to appear greedy.

"Freddie, this is home!" His aunt laughed. "You don't have any reason to put on airs here. Boy, give me a couple of minutes and I'll have that cheeseburger ready, okay?"

Mumbling a mild, thoroughly unconvincing protest, Fred Rawlings sat patiently, listening to the sounds of his aunt cooking behind him, and breathing in the wonderful aroma of another cheeseburger sizzling its way to medium-well.

Rubbing his head again for the second time since their encounter, his aunt placed a steaming cheeseburger in front of Fred Rawlings, got another glass of chocolate milk for him and sat down at the table again.

She seems mighty interested in watching me eat today, Fred Rawlings thought as he wolfed down the third burger, which barely had time to cool before vanishing into his gullet.

"Fred," Brenda Rawlings said, a question in her voice. "How are you doing with the girls at school—other than Chante Bates, I mean?"

"Whaddaya mean, Aunt Brenda?" Fred Rawlings replied, a chocolate-milk mustache gracing his upper lip.

"Look, Freddie, for one thing, I'm not that much older than you are. Just call me plain ol' Brenda, okay?"

Frowning, he lowered his glass back onto the table. He had always called her Aunt Brenda—what was wrong with that now? Plus, she was eighteen years older than he was, so what did she mean, she wasn't that much older?

"And I'll stop calling you Freddie and start calling you Fred. You're practically a man now." She paused. "Have you been with a woman yet, Fred?"

The question was so unexpected, Fred Rawlings nearly spewed chocolate milk across the table. "W-w-whaddaya mean, A-aunt Brenda? Do I be knowin' some women? Well, yeah. You know."

"Stop calling me Aunt Brenda," his aunt replied. There was the slightest hint of sharpness in her voice. "You make me feel old when you call me that. Do I look old to you?"

"Naw, naw, Aun—I mean, Brenda," Fred Rawlings said. "Some of my crew keep asking how old you are. They thought you went to our school." Averting his eyes, he blushed. "Some of my boys say they'd like to get with you," he said in a low, menacing voice, thinking about how he would like to crush their heads for even thinking about it.

Brenda Rawlings got up from her seat, stood behind her nephew and lightly placed her hands on his shoulders. His body felt like a granite outcropping, hard and unyielding beneath his shirt. Her last vestiges of inhibition vanished on the spot.

Grabbing her nephew's hand, Brenda Rawlings motioned for him to get up from the table. "Come here," she said, leading him toward her bedroom. "I want to show you something." She felt his hand pull back slightly.

"What's that, Aunt Brenda?" He quickly clapped his hand over his mouth. It would be hard not to put "aunt" before her name.

"Something you've never seen before," Brenda Rawlings said, ignoring the gaffe. "Something that you'll like a lot… and that you *need*, Fred."

Fred Rawlings's hand felt tense as his aunt led him into the bedroom and closed the door. "Fred, I care about you a great deal. You know that, right?"

"Y-y-yeah, I know that," he stammered, his slow brain finally realizing something was afoot. "What's goin' on, Aun—I mean, what's going on, Brenda?" The second time he said her name, his voice sounded slightly anxious. He had to be dreaming.

"Fred, when you drove a car for the first time, did you know what to do?" she asked, sitting down on her bed and pulling her nephew down beside her. "No!" she said, not waiting for an answer. "You had to get used to the brakes and what it felt like to turn the wheel, because it was all new to you, right?"

"Yeah, b-b-but—"

"Sex is no different, Fred," Brenda Rawlings said softly. "It's no different. If you're like most men, you won't know what to do, how to give a woman pleasure the first time you make love. Or, if you're like some men," she added, laughing easily, "the twenty-first time or the hundred-and-first."

Despite being nearly in a state of shock, Fred Rawlings marveled at his aunt's ability to be nonchalant as she set about the business of seducing him. He was anything but nonchalant. Especially when she unbuttoned her blouse and undid her bra, revealing her breasts. Fred Rawlings's eyes nearly popped out of his head.

Part of him wanted to stumble from the bedroom as quickly as possible. But the reptilian side of his brain made him stay put, mesmerized as it was by the sight of a partially nude woman.

And not just any woman, but Aunt Brenda, who had always resided on the loftiest of pedestals.

Before he knew it, she was guiding his hand toward her left breast. He reflexively yanked it away and jumped up from the bed.

She merely smiled and tilted her head back slowly, until her eyes locked on his. "What's the matter, Fred, you afraid of girls?" she asked, still grinning. "Tell you what, let's forget this ever happened, okay?"

"No, I ain't afraid of no girls," Fred Rawlings replied hotly. His aunt laughed out loud. She could make a black man do practically anything by pricking his ego—it was amazing how early that trait began to manifest itself.

"What's so funny?" Fred Rawlings asked defensively.

"Nothing, Fred," she said, starting to put her bra back on. "I just never dreamed you would be afraid of girls, that's all."

"I'm *not* afraid of no girls," he said, clumsily groping her left breast.

She closed her eyes, excited by his rough, awkward touch. He had an urgency in his hands that was electric.

"Fred, you have to be gentle with women," she said, opening her eyes and gently rubbing her brown, erect nipple with his huge fingers. Moving deliberately, belying the building excitement she felt, Brenda Rawlings got up from the bed and took her garments off, one at a time. She neatly folded each one and laid it on the bed. Slowly. Mustn't yield to instant gratification.

Fred Rawlings found his aunt's body more beautiful, more exquisitely proportioned, than anything he'd seen in *Playboy*. And she was actually there in the flesh, not some two-dimensional fantasy anchored to a piece of paper.

"Touch me here," his aunt said in a low growl as she stood beside her bed and parted her pubic hair with his hand. He did as he was told, this time with little reluctance.

"Gently, Fred. It's not a football—gently!" He carefully caressed and stroked her for a couple of minutes, when he began to notice an odd catch had appeared in her voice. "That's, uh, how you do it, Fred—uh! You learn real fast. Take your clothes off, please."

He stripped and stood in the middle of Brenda Rawlings's bedroom, his body that of a muscular, bronzed god. Even his nose guard had the appearance of something an African deity might wear. But she gasped when she glanced between Fred Rawlings's legs—he had a monstrous appendage unlike anything she'd ever seen.

And it was impatiently straining skyward.

Too aroused to move slowly anymore, Brenda Rawlings stood directly in front of Fred. "Pick me up," she said. He put his hands under her arms and easily elevated her inches from the ceiling.

"Now, let me down slowly." Brenda Rawlings was nearly panting with excitement at the thought of being impaled by that *thing!* It was as if the rest of Fred wasn't even in the room. As she wrapped her legs around the small of his back and locked her ankles, she couldn't stop staring at his groin.

She could barely get her fingers around the object of her attention as she guided it to a place unlike any it had ever been. Fred had barely gotten all the way in when he started shuddering, tossing Brenda Rawlings about like a small skiff on a choppy sea.

"Don't stop, Fred," she said, nearly coming herself as she watched his blissful expression. "Keep going." She had been seventeen once herself, and she knew Fred would have no problem maintaining his erection and continuing. Which was the case.

Instead of feeling guilty about what was happening, Brenda Rawlings felt proud. She was teaching something sacred and beautiful to someone she cared about deeply. It was better that he learn it from her than some fast little slut who might leave him with AIDS or a snot-nosed baby.

Here, he could learn everything he needed to know, free of pressure or expectations.

From Fred Rawlings's vantage point, he was being "rewarded" for trying to take care of Darryl Billups.

The lesson/reward session went on for an hour, ending with an admonishment from Brenda Rawlings: Fred, this is our little secret, all right? No one else needs to know about this, *especially* your mother, because she wouldn't understand.

CHAPTER THIRTY

I don't have a thing to say to Mad Dawg in the *Herald*'s elevator as we head back to the newsroom from the cafeteria. He's quiet, too, following our less than auspicious intro to the *Herald*'s new managing editor.

Mad Dawg has a heart of gold, as demonstrated by his help when I was in Atlanta. It's just that at times the brother doesn't know when to shut his mouth, making me feel like I could pop him upside his dreadlocked head.

Personal embarrassment aside, I'm thrilled Florence Newsome is coming here. The *Herald* has marginalized Baltimore's African-American community for more than a century—maybe she will finally bring that shameful practice to a halt.

As the elevator door glides open, Tom Merriwether and Cornelius Lawrence stroll past in the hallway. Both are wearing dark brown wing tips, blue Oxford shirts and brown slacks, and walk with matching tight-ass gaits. Scary. Actually, "sickening" is the word that best describes the lengths Cornelius goes through to ape his white supervisors.

Ignoring Mad Dawg, Merriwether looks at me. "Come on into my office, please, Darryl," he says quietly. I glance at

Cornelius, but his face is neutral and unreadable. He's absorbing his lessons well.

Hoping this isn't about the missing laptop, I look at Mad Dawg and follow Tomelius. They usher me into the office of managing editor Walter Watkins and Tom casually sits behind Watkins's desk. He reminds me of a little kid playing at being managing editor.

"Darryl, your coverage has been fabulous, right on the money," he says grandly, as if his assessment is a valuable yardstick. He's never gone out of his way to say nice things to me prior to the Confederate flag story. Wondering if his actions are in reaction to Florence Newsome's arrival, I smile. Naturally, he mistakes that for a positive response to his words.

"We need you to cover something related to the killings," Cornelius says, at ease ordering reporters around after nearly a year on the job. Except for the *Herald*'s select bunch of white prima donnas, of course, whom Cornelius practically approaches on his knees. He'd better not lose sight of the fact I'm going to be an editor again when this story concludes.

"What's up, Cornelius?" I say, glancing at my watch. Time is wasting—I could be out trying to find Cynthia Travers instead of sitting around here.

"The Reverend Royce Stephens is holding a meeting about the killings at his church in half an hour," Tom says, finishing Cornelius's thought. They do that quite a bit.

"We were wondering if you could run on down there and cover it for us."

The good reverend scares the living feces out of the *Herald*, which he frequently castigates as being racist and insensitive. Loudly. With sweat streaming down his face and onto his collar.

Whenever the *Herald* needs a quote from one of Baltimore's so-called "black leaders," Stephens's phone is guaranteed to remain quiet.

"I really need to do some background work on the Confederate flag story," I answer innocently.

Cornelius glances at Tom.

Tom abruptly thrusts a flier into my hand. "The meeting starts in about twenty-five minutes, Darryl."

To press my point home any further would just brand me as having a "bad attitude." For some reporters, doing the same thing would make them spirited and feisty—they'd have "pluck." But woe to the brother possessing "a bad attitude." It can be a career killer.

Thinking about what my Aunt Mimi says about "pick your battles," I leave Watkins's office. And motor on down to Stephens's church on Pennsylvania Avenue, feeling like a white-collar prostitute.

A surprisingly large early afternoon crowd is seated in the Church of the Holy Redeemer Baptist Church, ready and willing to be whipped into a state of righteous indignation by a man who excels at it. Personally, I think Stephens performs a useful service by keeping the *Herald* and other media outlets on their toes.

I also think Stephens is an opportunist who mostly cares more about his personal aspirations than God or his congregation. I also think he's a crook, even though he was acquitted of mail fraud and income tax charges in a spectacular trial that took place three years ago.

Now, he's supposed to be mulling a run for Congress. Whatever he's up to, the Reverend Stephens is never dull. And he definitely knows how to pull the strings of the media—right now his beautifully finished church is filled with jostling television, radio and newspaper reporters.

In the back of the church, alone and wearing sunshades, is detective Scott Donatelli. Since Stephens isn't supposed to get started for five minutes and is invariably ten to fifteen minutes late, I walk to the back and sit beside Scott.

He's not exactly inconspicuous, with his long hair, toothpick and white skin as he sits in the last pew of the Church of the Holy Redeemer Baptist Church in the heart of inner-city Baltimore.

"Got some news for you," he says, lifting his shades slightly and peeping under them. "We did a super rush job on Moore and Cooper's autopsy results, including toxicology. We didn't find a damned thing," Scott says in a perplexed tone. "Nothing!"

Craning my head toward the ceiling, where there's an awesome mural featuring a black Jesus, I rub my neck. "So what's your theory?" I inquire with practiced casualness, secretly dismayed no official cause of death has been discovered yet.

His only reply is a resigned shrug. I know the pressure on him must be tremendous. And it will only get worse by the time Stephens finishes his performance.

Feeding off the expectant buzz in the air, the reverent Reverend Stephens takes to the stage and stands behind a gleaming pine podium bristling with microphones. Feeling every eye in the house upon him and loving it, Stephens calmly walks to a small circular table holding a pitcher of water and a glass. He theatrically pours himself some water and sips it slowly, expertly milking the sense of anticipation inside the Church of the Redeemer.

A small, dark-skinned man in his fifties who photographs larger and younger than he is, Stephens smoothly draws a white handkerchief from the lapel of his navy blue, pinstriped double-breasted Italian suit.

"Tell is like it is, Reb," a portly man in the second pew shouts, beginning to clap rhythmically. The beat spreads to a couple more people on the man's pew and in no time the entire church is rocking.

Delighted, Stephens smiles without showing his teeth, then slowly raises his right hand for silence. "The reason I called this press conference," he says, dabbing his already glistening forehead, "is to expose a double-standard, a mockery, a travesty, a sham that puts—" he pauses dramatically in the television lights. "The life of every African-American in this city in jeopardy," he says, lowering his voice to a near whisper.

"Do you think for one second that-uh...Jews could be killed in this city-uh..."

"Preach, Reb."

"All right, now. That's what I'm talking about," a voice yells from Stephens's increasingly agitated audience.

"...and SWASTIKAS could-uh be placed on their heads-uh," Stephens roars in his richly textured baritone, sending the crowd into a frenzy. "And the police wouldn't have a suspect-uh? DO YOU?"

"Tell it like it is, pastor!"

It's already obvious to me that Stephens doesn't have much to say, he's just generating attention-getting sound bites. Even by his standards, today's performance is cynical.

An old time Baptist revival is building steam inside the Church of the Redeemer. Despite themselves, the white reporters present sneak nervous glances at each other as the intensity level rises.

By now, Stephens is practically shuddering, bellowing, moonwalking his way around the stage, flinging droplets of perspiration from his moisture-soaked clothes. He and his followers will shout and pray the Confederate flag killer into the open, into a confession and into the penitentiary, by God!

Smiling, I glance over my shoulder to see what's happening behind me. Looking thoroughly unmoved, shades firmly in place, Donatelli takes in the show from the back pew. He nods slightly in my direction, then gets up and walks toward the foyer, in search of the collection basket, no doubt.

CHAPTER THIRTY-ONE

Sitting at my computer back at the *Herald*, trying to think of a way to write about the Reverend Stephens that doesn't make him seem buffoonish, it suddenly hits me: I think I know how the Confederate flag victims have been killed! It's a wild guess, but it's as much as anyone else has to go on right now.

I make a note to myself to call the public relations department at the University of Maryland Shock Trauma Center, as well as Scott Donatelli. He may be able to show me something from the police evidence room that might corroborate my theory.

I write the Stephens story quickly so I can hurry up and get out of here and test my theory, as well as follow up on an action plan I've formulated. Basically, I am going to each and every pharmacist and gastroenterologist on that list that Donatelli gave me.

My plan is to enter the premises and see if I spot Cynthia Travers at work. If not, I'll hold up her picture from Atlanta and ask if any employee resembles it. I'll start within the inner city and work my way out to the suburbs.

As I put the finishing touches on the Stephens piece, the phone rings. It's Scott Donatelli, sounding excited.

"Hey, Sherlock Holmes, want to sit in on a stakeout? I think we have a strong suspect here." He spits out a rendezvous spot in North Baltimore and hangs up.

Pushing the SEND button that ships my story off to my editors, I yell across the newsroom about needing to talk to the police, then jog toward the elevators, throwing my overcoat on as I go.

Fiercely uncoordinated, uglier than two miles of dirt road, skinny and slew-footed, Dr. Roland Evans is actually picking his nose as he makes his way toward the disguised Baltimore City police van, where I sit watching him through high-powered binoculars.

"You think *this* guy is the Confederate flag killer?" I ask Donatelli, who has a pair of binoculars, too. "He's a bogeyman, all right—but a hardened killer? He looks like he would have trouble tying his shoes."

Two other cops in the van snicker. "How would you know what a killer looks like until we bring him in?" one of the cops sneers. "I told you not to bring Clark Kent," he says to Donatelli.

"He's cool," Scott says, never changing his expression.

"Evans still looks like a dork to me," I offer, grinning as I continue to squint through the binoculars. We're sitting at the end of the block in a working-class black neighborhood, in a van painted to look like a cable-repair vehicle.

Needling these cops helps break up the incredible boredom of a stakeout—we've been sitting here more than two hours waiting for Evans to leave the row house of a lady friend. And now he's finally walking toward his black Lincoln Continental Town Car, holding a black medical bag.

One of a handful of black gastroenterologists in the state, Evans went to Northwestern High in Baltimore around the same time Moore and Cooper did. Plus, within twenty-four hours of the estimated times of death for Moore and Cooper, Evans unexpectedly took off from his Baltimore County medical practice. Without explanation both times—he just canceled all his appointments.

When I asked if that was all these three cops had to go on, they traded knowing looks and said nothing.

"You'd think a doctor, of all people, would have more couth than to walk down the street with his finger jutting out of his nose," Scott says.

"Why?" One of his partners laughs. "They can be just as ill-mannered and disgusting as anyone else."

"Worse," the third cop chimes in.

Evans deposits his black medical bag in the trunk of his Lincoln, looks around three times, then walks back up the street and scurries up the steps of his lady friend's house.

If anything, it's gotten colder than it was this morning, when those snow flurries fell. Yet the front door is wide open. Evans disappears inside and runs back out immediately, struggling with a blue plastic hanging bag that appears to have a limp human form inside.

Evans more drags than carries the bag, which strikes each of the steps leading from the front door to the sidewalk.

"Looks like a body's in there," I note in an alarmed voice.

"Sure does," Donatelli says, starting the van's engine. "Let's roll, boys."

When we cruise up beside Evans's Lincoln and block his exit, he looks close to shitting bricks. The cops come bounding out immediately, guns drawn. I wait a split second before following, just in case shots are fired.

"Oh, God, no, please!" a whiny, nasal voice implores. "What do you guys want, money? I'll give you whatever you need, but please, please don't jeopardize my medical practice. I'll pay you whatever you want, just don't make me lose my license."

"Turn the car off," Donatelli barks. "Keep your hands where I can see them and get out slowly."

Doc Evans starts sobbing like Chris Darden. "Please, please," he cries, immediately throwing dignity to the wind. "Is it cash you need? How much? I can get it for you—within an hour."

"Hey, Scott, come look at this," one of Donatelli's partners says in a concerned voice as he peers into the trunk of Evans's car. I walk back with Donatelli to see the head of a blond, blowup sex doll peeking out of Evans's hanging bag.

"Go knock on the door of the house and make sure everybody is all right," Donatelli says disgustedly. A tired-looking woman angrily answers.

Glad that I don't have to deal with this foul-up, or its paperwork, I hide out in the warm van and watch the sunset while waiting for Donatelli and friends to wrap up.

CHAPTER THIRTY-TWO

The real Confederate flag killer sat on the floor of her apartment wearing an oversized electric-blue Chesapeake Bay T-shirt, with her knees drawn up tightly against her chest. Feeling filthy.

Two showers hadn't helped. Nor had her old staple—a large glass of Absolut and orange juice. An ugly six-letter word beginning with I and N and C was fighting to take root in her consciousness. And Brenda Rawlings was stubbornly trying to resist.

No more standing in judgment of people and glibly slapping labels on them. "You're not a rapist and you have not committed incest," Rawlings kept repeating to herself softly. "You are human and so is Fred and no one got hurt."

The old Brenda Rawlings wouldn't have done it. Wouldn't have dreamed of it. And if she had, would have beaten herself to death in an orgy of self-flagellation. *Well, I am not going to do that. Society can kiss my natural black ass.*

Clucking her tongue, she recalled how she'd naively believed that visiting Trudy would obliterate *The Presence*, stop its unpredictable comings and goings. Well, it was back. Bigger and more forceful than ever. Telling her to put her burgundy crushed-velvet hunting dress in the cleaners. Because she would need it soon. Possibly tomorrow.

You make me feel all this stuff—why couldn't you have made me leave Freddie alone? Damn you!

Feeling a familiar crawly sensation, Rawlings hopped to her feet and started moving toward the bathroom. Her period was on the way.

Good. It would give her an excuse to take a third shower—maybe this one would finally wash away that nasty feeling.

CHAPTER THIRTY-THREE

"D'ya hear the one," Scott Donatelli begins, slurring his words, "about the Chinaman, Irishman and the brother in the pickle factory?" He grins, tickled by the joke he's about to let fly. Except this knee-slapper ain't seeing the light of day with me around.

"Hate to be a party pooper, man," I say, holding up my hand and slurring my words a little, too, "but I don't do racial jokes."

"Do tell?" Donatelli says, comically gaping his mouth with exaggerated surprise. He's knocked back five tequila shooters in less than half an hour inside the Sportsman's Lounge, a black, gutbucket bar on Gwynn Oak Avenue in Northwest Baltimore featuring local jazz musicians. Scott is really trying to drink away the frustration of staking out a suspect who murdered a blow-up sex doll. Screwed it to death, I think.

When he invited me along, I agreed reluctantly. Any other night but tonight. This is an excellent opportunity to get to know him, but I'd much rather be home playing with Jamal and making up with my woman.

"Ya know what I think?" Donatelli says, drawing back indignantly, his eyes pink slits, "Huh? Bet if I was one of the brothers, you'd let me tell jokes all night. Allll damn night!"

"Be quiet, dammit! I'm trying to hear the woman sing!" growls a gruff, older black man wearing a checkered jacket at the table next to us. His female partner fixes Donatelli with a what's-he-doing-here? glare. The night is going downhill rapidly. The two cops who were with Donatelli on the stakeout, one of whom is black, are both as drunk as he is.

"Am I disturbing you, sir?" Donatelli says, sweeping back his jacket about a third of an inch, just enough for his gun holster to show. "Sir, I am so terribly sorry. Tell me, would you like to talk about race?"

The black man at the next table looks at Donatelli like he's lost his mind, which I'm starting to think may not be that far-fetched a thought.

"Come on," the woman says, still glaring at Donatelli as she and her partner get up and move to another table.

Giving a little snorting laugh that indicates he couldn't give a damn, Donatelli holds his shot glass up to the light and studies it intensely. "What is it with you guys?" he says in a quiet voice, still looking up at his glass. "Does it make you uncomfortable to talk to a white boy about race?"

My eyes are aflame from cigarette smoke, I'm tired, tipsy, and yeah, he's right. I don't like talking to whites about race. Particularly under circumstances like this where alcohol is in the mix, raising the potential for an inflammatory, insensitive gaffe.

Under the best of circumstances, I feel like everybody is going to go home with his perspective firmly intact and possibly some bruised feelings. Anyway, it's a rare white person who harbors a genuine interest in the experience of people who look like me.

"First of all, who does 'you guys' refer to?" I ask Donatelli, who slowly lowers his head and bores his eyes into mine. "Let me tell you something, Scott. African-Americans don't appreciate being referred to as 'you guys' or 'you people.'"

The black cop nods vigorously.

"Anyway," I say, noticing to my horror that the worm is no longer in the tequila bottle and not being able to remember where it went, "it's stupid conversation, if you think about it. Basically, it boils down to, I have a little more or less of a certain chemical in my skin than you do. Isn't that some silly shit? That's what any racial discussion between a black person and a white person really boils down to. We could just as easily talk about how your ears are bigger than mine."

"Come here," Donatelli says, waggling his finger in an admonishing way. I lean toward him.

"Lighten up, my friend!" he bellows. "It's all bullshit, just something to talk about. Like talking about baseball."

It's a helluva lot more than just bullshit, or some dumb-ass game. But like I already told him, I'm not getting drawn into it. Not here, not tonight.

"Nothing personal, okay, buddy?" Donatelli says, sticking out his hand. "Lemme tell you somethin', but if you repeat it I'll deny it," he says, giving me a booming clap on the shoulder. "You're one pretty good reporter, Darryl Billups. You don't know shit about picking murder suspects, going after pretty little women and all, but you're good at what you do. And I like you."

He raises his glass to the ceiling. "Here's to Darryl Damn Billups!" he roars as his partners dissolve into laughter.

"Shhhh! Shhhh! Shhhh!"

Everyone is cutting his eyes at us now.

I laugh as I raise my glass. "You're something else, Scott. I'm not sure what, but you're something else, baaabeeee."

Now even the jazz singer and her three-piece band are flinging daggers our way. Time to shut down this male-bonding session and go home. If I can manage to drive my car five blocks, that is.

CHAPTER THIRTY-FOUR

Man is a creature of habit, so it's said, and I'm no exception.

I'm so used to coming and going when I please, I didn't give a second thought to rolling into the house semi-drunk at 1:25 in the morning. And then turning on the stereo, although not all that loud.

The truth of the matter is, force of habit and several shots of tequila made me forget Yolanda and Jamal were even here. I can't use that same excuse for failing to call her all day or not buying some flowers, in light of our little blowup. I really did mean to, though, for what that's worth.

I'm bumbling around in the kitchen, trying to make a sandwich and making more noise than anything, when Yolanda shuffles around the corner, barefoot and dressed in pajamas. And looking like she could bite the heads off nails.

"Hey, baby," she says in a gravelly voice, looking at me closely. In a way that silently inquires, "Have you lost your mind, good brother?"

"Baaaaabeeee," I slur, exhaling a cloud of noxious tequila fumes. "Been thinkin' 'bout you all day." That sentiment is capped off with a sloppy kiss on the side of Yolanda's pretty head.

"Darryl...are you drunk?"

"Meeeee! Puhleeeeze. You ever seen me drunk afore? I'm just feeling good and glad to see my baaaabeeee." That's followed by another wet kiss Yolanda disgustedly wipes away. Looking annoyed, she clicks off the stereo, right in the middle of a tune by one of my favorite Brazilian jazz artists.

"Come on, boy," she says, crossing her arms and causing her nipples to poke through her shirt. "Let's put your behind in bed."

"Lawd hab mussy. That a imbitation o' sumpfin?"

Yolanda laughs. "Negro, please! You'll be lucky to stay awake past the bedroom door."

"We'll see 'bout dat," I respond, walking on rubbery legs as Yolanda pulls me out of the kitchen. "You in trouble now."

I collapse on the bed as soon as we reach the bedroom and start snoring like a beast before Yolanda can even yank my shoes off.

True love manifests itself in a number of ways. Forget about violins and flowers—true love is when a woman climbs out of her comfortable bed at four in the morning to comfort your ashy, hungover butt while you retch your brains out.

Looking bleary-eyed and concerned, Yolanda sits on the side of the bathtub and tenderly pats my back as I kneel before the commode begging forgiveness for my debauchery. My stomach is a rumbling volcano threatening to explode from both ends, while a buzz saw cruelly ricochets inside my head, reducing my brain to slivers of confetti.

I think I'm still nineteen, capable of hanging out with the boys all hours of night, drinking like a fish, enjoying three orgasms a night, dunking a basketball without warming up first. Lately, however, my body is increasingly reminding me that it's thirty-three.

"I'm sorry, Yolanda," I mumble with embarrassment, finally able to raise my head for a second or two. "Why don't you go on back to bed?"

"Stop talking, Darryl," she scolds. "As soon as you get that rotgut out of your body, I got some bicarbonate of soda for you."

As the volcano gets ready to fire up again, I feel Yolanda's hands gently massaging my back. I know at that instant that I'm going to ask this woman to marry me—I'd be a damn fool to let Yolanda get away.

CHAPTER THIRTY-FIVE

"So, what's it gonna be, Scott? You gonna catch the Confederate flag killer today, or what?"

Donatelli evilly glances up from a scalding cup of coffee whose steam caresses his face and oozes through his hair. He looks just like I feel—like five miles of bad road. His face is stubble-flecked, bluish-black shadows hug the corners of his bloodshot eyes and his brow is creased irritably.

"What?" he barks loudly, his voice sounding like a nuclear detonation to my hungover ears.

"Keep your voice down," I growl, not in a mood to take crap from anybody this morning. If I weren't covering this case, I definitely would have called in sick.

We're seated in the same hole-in-the-wall Baltimore Street cafe where Donatelli and I met right after Phil Gardner went down with his perforated ulcer. Gardner's funeral is tomorrow, which probably further exacerbates Donatelli's agitated state.

Looking down at the floor, he exhales, puffing out his cheeks. If the tequila in his system is kicking his heinie anything like it's wearing out mine, he's a hurting pup right about now.

A white woman with a high, screechy voice at the table next to ours is prattling on and on about nothing, complaining about her boss, her boyfriend, the state of the union, life in general. Donatelli and I give each other insolent looks, annoyed by the nonstop, high-decibel assault.

"'Scuse me, miss," he finally says, flashing his badge. "Is that your blue convertible by that parking meter?"

She stares at him indignantly and doesn't reply.

"Well, you can't park beside that meter until nine A.M.," he continues gruffly. "That's twenty minutes from now. I would suggest you move that vehicle if you don't want a citation."

"Why don't you go arrest some murderers or muggers or something?" the woman says huffily rising from her chair, and leaving a half-eaten bagel behind. Slamming down three dollar bills on her table, and making Scott and me wince, she storms out the door and drives away.

"Thank you," I say softly, staring into the bottom of my coffee mug. The headache tablets I popped half an hour ago haven't kicked in and I ain't moving till they do. I've definitely gotta stop what feels and sounds like a waterfall of pain inside my head.

"We need some of the hair of the dog that bit us," Donatelli says in a near whisper. Then, very offhandedly, he adds, "I think we may have another suspect soon."

"Oh, really? Who?"

"A low-level bureaucrat in the mayor's office."

I hate being teased like that. "Who, Scott?"

"Can't say just yet. But I should be able to say shortly. And what about you, Sherlock? What's on your agenda today?"

"I'm going to hit all those pharmacies and stomach doctors on your list," I tell him, waiting for the inevitable ribbing about Cynthia Travers.

"Well, good luck, then," Donatelli says, holding up his coffee mug chest-high. "May the best man win."

"No, may the best *men* win. There's no reason for this to be a contest.

Donatelli just smiles. This is going to be a pride thing to the end with him—he isn't going to work with me under any circumstances. But come to think of it, I wouldn't particularly want to write a story with him, either.

The digital pager the *Herald* has given to me starts beeping for the first time in about three weeks. Tom Merriwether's number shows up. Something really big must be up for him to be paging me before 9 A.M. I think as I walk to a pay phone inside the greasy spoon, right beside where the owner is shouting orders to his short-order cook.

"Hello," Merriwether says, sounding impatient.

"Hey, Tom. What's up?"

"Come to the office immediately."

"Why, what's going on? I was going to chase down some more leads."

"That can wait," Merriwether says in an obstinate tone. "In the meantime, I need to see you *right now!*"

The muscles in my stomach tighten as I hang up and return to my table, where Scott Donatelli is staring zombie-like at an ashtray.

"I gotta go, man," I tell him, swinging into a full-length black leather coat that makes me look and feel like Darth Vader. "But could you do me a favor? Could you tell me what was on that grocery receipt you guys found in Darcel Moore's bathroom?"

Merriwether and Cornelius Lawrence wait for me in the office of managing editor Walter Watkins, who is soon to be replaced by Florence Newsome. As before, Merriwether sits behind Watkins's huge desk, fantasizing about a position he'll never get if a meritocracy exists here.

"Where's the laptop you took to Atlanta, Darryl?" Merriwether begins. "Cornelius says it's no longer in your possession. That so?"

Cornelius grins smugly.

"That's right, Tom," I answer slowly, trying vainly to think of an explanation that puts a positive spin on Atlanta, but failing to find one. "I…was accused of sexual assault in Atlanta and they held my laptop for fingerprint evidence."

Tom and Cornelius are dumbfounded. "Jesus Christ, Darryl," Cornelius says in a shrill voice. "Do you think maybe you should have told us about this? I mean, the credibility of the entire paper is at stake—"

"That's right," Tom says, cutting in. "What on God's earth were you thinking, man? What do you think would have happened if the *Tribune* had found out about this, whether it's true or not?"

"I'm totally innocent, Tom. The whole thing is bullshit. The woman who made the accusation never even showed up to identify me in a lineup. No charges have been—"

"You were in a lineup?"

"Yes, but—"

"Have you lost your mind?" Cornelius blurts out.

"This is one of the more asinine lapses of judgment I've seen in quite some time," Merriwether says, excitedly stroking his chin with a scrawny hand. Cornelius, who's loyally standing behind Merriwether, looks like a kid on Christmas morning.

"Not only are you unfit to be an editor here, Darryl, I'm wondering if you even have what it takes to be a reporter," Merriwether says, stretching out his hand.

"Let me have your *Herald* ID," he demands.

I look at him in disbelief. Confiscating a journalist's ID is tantamount to yanking a policeman's badge.

"You're suspended, Darryl," Merriwether says calmly. "With pay, for the time being, until I have a chance to talk to Watkins. He should be in later this afternoon. Until then, you can go on home."

It seems like I'm watching a movie where someone else fishes a newspaper ID out of his wallet, gently lays it before Merriwether, then walks out of Watkins's office, out of the newsroom and out the front door of the *Herald*. The whole time I wait for someone to jump out and scream, "April Fool!"

No one does, so I get into my car and drive home.

CHAPTER THIRTY-SIX

Finding myself home unexpectedly, feeling numb and not really knowing what to do with myself, I turn on my personal computer. When the little Windows icons appear, I absently double-click on the one for solitaire and start playing. The computer wins the first game, making me wonder if maybe I should have stayed in bed today.

I deal the little cards again and play a second game that calls for me to maneuver the cards around a bit before I win. In the third game I just blow the computer away. Not till game four do I start getting pissed off.

What the hell are you doing here, Darryl? Are you going to sit around moping, playing solitaire and having a damn pity party just because Tom and Cornelius said to go home? Or are you going to do something that may help stop a killer?

I finish whipping the computer's butt a third straight time and shut it down. Fetching my Darth Vader coat from the closet, I toss it over my shoulders, grab my briefcase and head out the door.

Since I'm suspended, that means I can do whatever the hell I please. At the moment, I feel like going through every pharmacy and gastroenterologist's office in Baltimore, looking for Cynthia Travers.

I still have enough business cards to do that.

CHAPTER THIRTY-SEVEN

The pharmacist working at the Optima Pharmacy around the corner from my house appears to be from India and clearly enjoys his work. He and a pharmacy technician are laughing and joking as they go about the business of meticulously filling prescriptions, scraping technicolor pills into brown plastic vials and slapping labels on them.

He makes me wait for a couple of minutes, as pharmacists are wont to do, before finally coming over to see what I want.

"Good morning," he says cheerfully, eyes dancing behind a pair of bifocals. "What can I do for you, young man?"

"My name is Darryl Billups and I'm a reporter with the *Baltimore Herald*. I'm trying to locate somebody for a story I'm working on." I hold Cynthia Travers's picture up for him to see, and he takes off his glasses and tilts his head quizzically. If he asks for identification, I'll just hand him one of my business cards.

He smiles and shakes his head. "Nope, nobody working here that looks like that. Attractive young lady."

"Thanks for your time," I tell him as I slide the picture back in my briefcase and snap it shut. Before I leave, I grab an Optima Pharmacy brochure listing seven locations in the Baltimore metro area.

I'm going to canvass the pharmacies first, because they're easier to poke around in than doctors' offices. Near the front door, I open my briefcase again and check off pharmacy number one.

Only one hundred thirty-six more to go.

I'm oh for twenty-seven on my pharmacy search when my *Herald* pager starts beeping again. This time, it displays an unfamiliar number at the *Herald.*

Stopping at a phone booth in a particularly tough section of Northwest Baltimore, I call to see what new drama awaits.

"Good morning, Richmond—" a female voice says, pauses, then starts laughing. "I mean *Baltimore Herald.* Florence Newsome here."

"Hi, this is Darryl Billups," I say with a confident tone that belies the butterflies attacking my stomach.

"I'm so used to giving the name of my last paper—Darryl, swing by the *Herald.* We need to talk. Where are you?"

"Doing some digging on the Confederate flag story."

"How soon can you get down here?"

"I can be there in twenty minutes."

"Okay. I know you don't have an ID, so just ask for me at the guard's desk."

When I get to the fifth floor of the *Herald*, Florence Newsome is going over some paperwork in an unused office filled with packing crates. She's so engrossed she doesn't glance up for several seconds after I knock on the door and enter.

"Have a seat over there," she says in a preoccupied way, pointing toward a chair with a thin layer of dust on it, near the desk where she's seated. "This will only take another second or two." I wait patiently, feeling like I'm in the principal's office.

"Soooo, Darryl," Newsome finally says, looking up. "What happened in Atlanta?"

I tell her everything that went down, including dinner at the Prime Rib and being asked to stand in a lineup.

"Anything else?" Newsome asks sharply. "Were any charges filed? Or are they pending?"

"No. That's everything that happened."

Newsome unconsciously pokes her tongue out as she vigorously erases something on the paper in front of her. Then she focuses fully on me for the first time.

"You're a fine reporter, Darryl," she says with that hard-edged attentiveness strong personalities generate. "I've reviewed your clips and I certainly know your work with the NAACP story. But at the end of the day, you and your friend—the one I met in the cafeteria the other day—could benefit from some discretion. Are we on the same wavelength?"

"Yes. Yes, we are."

Newsome's face softens somewhat. "Between you, me and the fence post, there are going to be some changes around here. Tom Merriwether and Cornelius Lawrence will probably be reassigned to other duties. But I think you might make a good manager if you work at it, Darryl. Your editing position is still yours to reclaim, if that's what you decide to do."

"Thank you," I say gratefully. "I'm glad to hear that."

She switches her attention back to her paperwork, allowing several moments of silence to pass.

"Why are you still here?" she asks, not bothering to look up and smiling slightly. "Don't you have a big story to chase? Oh, by the way—make sure that four-thousand-dollar laptop of yours is back in Baltimore within a week, or else give me a very good explanation why it's not. Bye."

I happily depart the *Herald*—ID in hand—and continue my search. By the time I knock off for the day, I've come up empty in fourteen more pharmacies, bringing the total to forty-one.

CHAPTER THIRTY-EIGHT

Spinning and primping gaily in front of a full-length mirror, Brenda Rawlings was reminded of that silly cereal commercial where a shapely white woman in a red mini-dress prances mindlessly in front of a mirror, in love with herself.

You're a cereal killer, Brenda.

For some reason, Rawlings found that image hysterically funny, making her décolletage shimmy inside her crushed burgundy dress. Her hunting togs.

Her power was off the register tonight. She was 120 pounds of brown dynamite. Samson had his hair and Brenda Rawlings had her burgundy Donna Karan.

Woe to anything or anyone foolhardy enough to oppose her.

Standing still momentarily, she took a long glance at the woman staring back. A handsome being with devastating curves, a pretty face and a confident, take-charge mien. A go-getter—maybe a top executive at a Fortune 500 company. Or the owner of a successful business.

Not the timid doormat who bought sensible clothes on sale, religiously squirreled away ten percent of her meager paychecks and flossed after every damn meal. And who forever danced a razor's edge, trying to please and accommodate and never offend.

Well, she was on hiatus tonight, off in Milquetoastland or wherever the hell she had disappeared to.

The brown bomber vamping in the burgundy dress hated her with a purple passion. Miss How-Will-I-Bend-Over-and-Let-the-World-Screw-Me-Today? One of these days, the bomber was going to ransack the apartment and burn all of the mousy Brenda's wholesome, boorrrrrinng clothes.

And then sit and wait, *daring* her to return.

Fetching a tube of burgundy lip gloss, she stood about two inches from the mirror. The killing zone. Once anyone got that close, it was all over. Except for Darryl Billups, who was undoubtedly gay.

"That's the only way any man could pass on this," Rawlings said, puckering her lips. Men are so *stupid*—once their testosterone is percolating, they never notice a calculating mind filled with bad intentions.

She envisioned idiotic Darcel Moore roasting in hell, still trying to figure out how he got there. "Little ol' Brenda would never do anything to me," Rawlings said, imitating Moore's baritone.

Well, soon enough Darcel would be talking with Lydell King, a man with a beautifully appropriate surname. Because he was king of the pigs. Brenda the Meek had put up with his infuriating groping when she worked for him a year ago. Hell, Brenda the Meek had blamed herself—as usual—for his loutish behavior.

He was smugly certain Rawlings had come to her senses by asking to cook dinner for him at his place tonight. But the ultimate treat would be to watch him die.

CHAPTER THIRTY-NINE

Sitting on a threadbare, blue cloth sofa in the living room, I work at massaging my way back into Yolanda's good graces, slowly rubbing the balls of her feet. No question I'm working hard at earning brownie points here, because I don't like touching my own feet. Not only are they ugly, funky appendages, but they're fungi-prone, too.

Jamal sits hypnotized in front of the television, contently watching a silly, ultraviolent cartoon where characters are blowing each other up every thirty seconds. I feel that parents should guide their children toward electronic nourishment, instead of slop. That will be fodder for a future conversation—definitely not tonight.

Yolanda idly flips through an *Essence* magazine with E. Lynn Harris on the cover, pleased her manservant is on the case.

As for me, I'm not even in the room. I'm trying to put myself into the head of a black person who could indiscriminately kill black people. It's a mental trick that television sleuths seem to master all the time. I can't pull it off, however.

Self-loathing and moronic street machismo have turned gangbangers into the modern-day Klan—that I understand.

But the Confederate flag killer? It just doesn't click. Two black men, one black woman, all young professionals, all found in bathtubs...not clicking. Definitely not clicking.

"Hello! Darryl, you there?" Yolanda says. She's put her magazine on the coffee table and is staring at me oddly. "You've been rubbing the same foot in the same spot for ten minutes! What gives?"

"Sorry."

Yolanda smiles. "Brotherman, would you mind letting me in?" she says, curling up on my lap. "I feel like you live a secret life I'm not a part of."

As she says this, an orange cartoon cat streaks across the TV screen engulfed in flames as a mouse and a dog stand by, watching, laughing wildly. I frown, but keep my counsel.

"I'm just thinking about this story I'm working on... what would make somebody kill young black people for no apparent reason."

"That's what you racking your head over? You can't come up with a reason because whoever it is probably doesn't think normally, Darryl. If you did understand, I'd start worrying about *you!*"

For the past couple of days I have been mainlining on an adrenal rush that comes from chasing a real-life monster. I am totally engrossed and engaged—hell, I could go through about thirty more pharmacies right now if it weren't for the fact most of them are closed.

On a human level, the Confederate flag killings are horribly tragic. On a professional level, they're nirvana.

"Want anything from the fridge?" I ask Yolanda as I rise from the couch to get some juice.

"Naw, baby. I'm going to put Jamal to bed."

On my way to the kitchen, I deliberately stop right in front of the television, blocking Jamal's view of his beloved cartoon.

He swivels his head comically, even though I'm totally eclipsing the screen. "Move," he says with quiet irritation. Crouching down, still blocking the set, I start waving my arms like a matador, grinning all the while.

"Moooovvee," Jamal shrieks, enraged now.

Backing up, I intentionally bump into the on/off switch, turning the TV suddenly black and silent.

With a quickness that surprises me, Jamal charges, little arms flailing in a determined bid to knock me into the next century.

"Stop it, you two." Yolanda laughs, just as Jamal lands a haymaker on my right knee. These fights can be dangerous—a wicked punch to the family jewels brought one of our bouts to an abrupt, painful close.

"Oh, you want some of this, huh?" I growl, tackling Jamal and holding him down as I tickle him. "Boy, don't you know I've had my hands on Mommy's feet?" I yell, clasping a hand over his face. "Let's bring chemical warfare into this, chump!"

Jamal tries hard to stay serious and mad, but after I walk my fingers across his belly a couple of times, he's laughing hysterically as we wrestle on the floor.

"Children. *Children!*" Yolanda says. "Darryl, I've asked you not to get him riled up right before I put him to bed! It's hard enough getting him to sleep as it is."

"What does she know?" I ask Jamal, who's back on his feet and taking five punches for every one he manages to hit me with. Luckily for him, Mom comes to the rescue by sweeping him off his feet and carrying him off to bed.

Thirsty after my light workout, I head into the kitchen, where I can't find a clean glass to save my life. So I pour grape juice into a white porcelain mug. This habit drives Yolanda crazy—she says mugs are for coffee or tea. Period.

The dark juice flowing from the carton reminds me of blood, which in turn makes me think of Phil Gardner. His funeral is tomorrow. I don't want to go, because his death isn't real for me just yet. As long as I don't see him lying in a casket, I can keep clinging to comforting denial.

"I applied for nursing school today," Yolanda says, entering the kitchen after putting Jamal down for the night. Coming up behind me, she wraps her strong brown arms around my waist. I can feel her warm breath rustling the hairs on my neck.

"So what do you think?" I put my mug down and turn to face her.

"Well, it ain't gonna be no walk—I mean, it's not going to be a walk in the park. There are a lot of tough subjects and I'll probably have to do a lot of studying."

"You can do it," I tell her in a reassuring voice, then lean over and plant a kiss on her forehead.

She looks unconvinced. "I'm not stupid or nothin' like that," she says pensively. "It's just that, well, schoolwork has never been my strong point." Yolanda has worry lines running across her forehead and is actually biting her lower lip. I've never seen her like this before.

"Well, you did a year and a half at the Community College of Baltimore, right? And you got As and Bs while you were there, right?"

"Yeah, Darryl, but nursing school is different."

"Oh, really? How?"

"It's a professional school, Darryl! This isn't some easy junior-college deal—these classes are hard!"

"You know what I think?" I say, drawing her close. "I think I have more faith in your ability than you do. You know what else I think?"

"No. But you're going to tell me."

"That for anatomy class, you might need a tutor. And I hereby volunteer my services, madam—Darryl Billups, anatomy instructor extraordinaire."

"What do *you* know about anatomy?" Yolanda says, throwing her head back disdainfully and arching those wild eyebrows. "Aren't you the same professor who came in here last night bragging about your qualifications, then fell down on the job?"

Sliding my hands into the back pockets of Yolanda's jeans, I pull her close. "Look, I charge by the hour and you've already burned up fifty dollars." Grabbing her by the hand, I lead her toward the bedroom.

Nothing compares to the lovemaking that takes place after a spat.

CHAPTER FORTY

Unfortunately, a fancy title and a comfortable salary have transformed many black men into insufferable, pompous jackasses. Which was partially why pharmacist Lydell King believed he could freely fondle and otherwise harass Brenda Rawlings when she worked as his assistant.

And also why he never questioned the turnabout in her behavior when she magically appeared at his door lugging three large grocery bags. Smiling demurely and eager to cook dinner in his Pratt Street high-rise, with its panoramic view of the harbor.

Just a year prior, a spluttering, hysterical Brenda Rawlings had stridden into his office and turned in her resignation without warning or explanation. The act had stunned King, because it was so unlike Rawlings.

Now here she was tonight, the same petite vision of loveliness, with a pink overnight bag dangling at her side from a shoulder strap, in addition to the other stuff she was carrying.

This silly bitch has finally come to her senses, King thought, grandly offering his outstretched hand. *Because she knows damn well there aren't a lot of intelligent, successful, HIV-free single brothers like me on every corner.*

Tall and muscular, King had the kind of mulatto appearance that made black women swoon, even though most of them knew better. With sandy hair—naturally wavy "good" hair—keen features, bulging arms and chest, he was Baltimore's black Adonis. He cut a striking figure in his stone-washed jeans, black-banded collar shirt and sockless black Italian leather loafers, and he knew it.

His smug expression wasn't lost on Brenda Rawlings—it was a reaffirmation of her decision to come tonight. Not only hadn't he learned his lesson, he appeared to have gotten worse. But this time he wore the shit-eating grin of a doomed man.

She grinned back, pleased to have a deadly little secret her former boss wouldn't be able to guess in a million years. With the strange exception of Darryl Billups, killing was getting a little easier each time out. Dealing with King would be like swatting a nettlesome, high-yellow fly.

"Brenda, it's really good to see you again. Here, let me grab those for you," King said unctuously, reaching for the grocery bags. His action was borne less of chivalry than of a desire to get Rawlings out of her black trench coat so he could ogle her heavenly body once more.

But she surprised him by quickly withdrawing the bags, then stepping back so he couldn't peer into them. Cool. He'd already seen two bottles of Asti Spumante in one, so he didn't care about the others. She'd gone through the trouble of supplying the alcohol for her inevitable seduction. How considerate!

That meant King could save his expensive cognac for the bank vice president dropping by tomorrow.

"A girl's got to have her surprises," Rawlings said, smiling coquettishly. "I want what I prepare for you tonight to be a total surprise. I think," she added, pausing, "you'll find it quite enjoyable. Which way is the kitchen?"

She probably needs her job back, King thought.

Laughing a Lothario's easy chuckle, he bowed at the waist, stepped out of the doorway and pointed her toward his kitchen. Which was about as far as his knowledge of that strange place went—Lydell King couldn't find his way around it with a compass. Why did he need to, when some lovely young thing was always puttering around, whipping up delicacies for him?

Rawlings's meal would be the third one prepared for him this week. As he was fond of telling his boys, one day he would invite all his ho's over and they'd hold a bake-off.

As Brenda Rawlings sashayed by him, King never took his eyes off her rounded outline.

"Don't come in yet," she yelled from the kitchen. King heard the sound of the bags thumping to the kitchen floor, then bottles and containers being rearranged in his refrigerator as Rawlings put her food away.

"Why are you putting that stuff in the refrigerator?" he called out. "Aren't you going to cook it? There's plenty of space on the kitchen counter."

"Be patient, Lydell," she replied in a low, sexy voice. "I know what I'm doing. Just tell me where the champagne glasses are."

"Heh, heh, heh. In the cabinet over the stove, to the right."

Sitting in his dining room, which afforded a spectacular view of the merchant ships gliding into Baltimore's harbor, King looked out over the twinkling lights of the city and sighed contentedly. Most brothers would have to work hard just to get Rawlings's phone number, but all he had to do was sit back and await a booty call. "Heh, heh, heh."

"Lydell, which way is your guest closet?"

He was on his feet immediately, because unwrapping presents was half the fun. "Hold on, hold on." He got to the kitchen just in time to see Rawlings drape her trench coat over her left arm. The image of the burgundy dress seared itself into his frontal lobes and King was in a fog from that point forward, a total slave to his—nonthinking—head.

"Goddamn!" he heard himself blurt under his breath as he reached for Rawlings's coat, all pretense of suaveness momentarily shattered.

From then on, Rawlings saw that King would be no challenge at all. Disappointing in every other regard, he'd just served up one final letdown. Asshole!

"Life has been agreeing with you, I see," he said as he bent over and kissed her on the cheek. His touch broke the connection, sapped the power that had been exploding inside her up to that point. Sagging, Rawlings felt the corned beef sandwich she'd had for lunch rising in her throat.

"Which way is the bathroom?" she said in a hushed voice King mistook for sexy but was really Rawlings trying not to vomit all over his burnt-orange carpet.

Smiling, he took her coat and pointed toward a door in his sprawling, ostentatious palace, that was liberally decorated with macho leather and dark-colored woods.

Double-timing it, Rawlings slammed the door and gripped the sides of a black marble sink until her knuckles went white. She tasted corned beef and stomach acid that stung the back of her throat, but somehow managed not to upchuck. Lydell

King would have to be dealt with quickly—if his sorry ass touched her again, she would lose it.

He was standing outside the bathroom door when she opened it, looking expectant.

Sit your half-white-looking butt down, you big, slobbering simpleton.

"You okay?" Concern was etched all over his face—concern that something might throw a monkey wrench into his evening of fun.

"Lydell, go sit down at the dining room table," Rawlings said in a cheerful, tinkly voice. "I want to propose a toast."

She came back with an open bottle of Asti and said some nonsense about letting bygones be bygones, or some such. Her words weren't important; getting King to drink was. He never even noticed he drank most of the first bottle, while Rawlings had drunk only a glass and a half.

He was becoming more octopuslike with each passing glass, too, starting with a hand laid lightly on an arm, then on a shoulder; then "innocent" brushes against breasts; then a sweaty hand resting boldly on a thigh.

Rawlings gritted her teeth and kept smiling, kept making inane small talk. *Touch on, motherfucker!* After being felt up by this Neanderthal during the ten horrible months they had worked together, she could endure a few more minutes. He would never do that to her or anyone else after tonight.

Observing King closely, Rawlings daintily put her glass down, pretended to stretch and then brought her hand directly onto his crotch! Looking terribly startled and temporarily out of control, he sat bolt upright.

"You're a big boy," Rawlings purred, running her tongue across her lips several times. "And I'm a big girl. We both know this B.S. we're talking about isn't what's really on our minds."

King looked like a happy puppy about to fall over itself.

"I'm still going to cook you dinner, but can we fast-forward and go straight to dessert?"

"Yeeaaahh!" King leered, leaning over and roughly grabbing Rawlings's breasts, which were tender and swollen from her period. As pain shot through her chest, Rawlings smacked King's hands, hard.

The come-hither, sex-kitten voice was gone when she spoke next, replaced by one that snagged the inebriated King's full attention. "Look, we're going to do this *my* way," she said icily. "Got that? Do that again and I'm outta here."

"You gonna do that dominatrix thang on me, girl?" He laughed. "I'm sorry, I'll be a good boy." As he took another swig of sparkling wine, Rawlings quietly took several deep breaths.

"Tell you what, baby," she purred, back in character. "Let's do a freaky little bathtub thing. Why don't I run some bathwater and you can come in and join me in your birthday suit. But don't come until I tell you to, okay? I have a little outfit I want you to see."

King nodded and strolled toward his bedroom, congratulating himself. Mission accomplished! Watching him walk away, Rawlings shook her head. Then she entered the main bathroom, which was detached from the bedroom. A sunken tub made of black granite with gold fixtures dominated the room. Two marble steps led to the tub, which had whirlpool nozzles.

Leaning over the tub, Rawlings reached down and closed the drain, then turned on the water. She adjusted it so it was just slightly cooler than room temperature. With the water still running, Rawlings jogged into the kitchen and retrieved her black overnight bag. Then she opened the refrigerator and pulled out one of her grocery bags.

Returning to the bathroom, she placed her overnight bag beside the tub and hid the grocery bag in a cabinet under the sink.

"I'm ready now!" King shouted from behind his closed bedroom door.

"No, not yet! Give me five more minutes," Rawlings yelled back. Flying out of the bathroom, she returned to the kitchen, snatched the two remaining grocery bags from the refrigerator and slid them under the bathroom sink. Then she locked the door, slipped out of her burgundy dress and slithered into a yellow-gold teddy that left little to the imagination.

She slid the overnight bag across the bathroom floor with her left foot, then reverently laid her hunting dress over the bag. Once again, it had worked magnificently.

"Lydell," she cooed. "It's time now."

He ambled into the bathroom obviously aroused and wearing only jockey shorts, which he immediately flung toward the shower.

For the first time since her arrival, Rawlings enjoyed a genuine laugh. *You poor, self-absorbed bastard. You actually think this is about you! You actually think this is about sex!*

She started rubbing between her legs and moaning quietly, waiting for his predictable advance. "No, baby," she said, sounding near orgasm. "Why don't you get into the tub first? There's something I want to do to you."

Rawlings eagerly complied. Now the only question was, would she leave the Confederate flag decal on his forehead or do something different and plaster it across the bridge of his pointy nose?

"The water is cold!" King said in a whiny voice.

"It'll warm up shortly," Rawlings said cheerfully, pulling her teddy down to let King get a glimpse of her left breast. *Men are big babies—throw a little titty at them and they shut right up.*

"Time for a surprise," Rawlings said suddenly, grinning as she walked over to the light switch and snapped it off.

"Whaddaya doin'?"

"You'll see."

In the darkness, King heard a squeak as the cabinet door under the sink opened. Then he heard the rustling of plastic and paper, then the sound of bags being dragged across the bathroom floor toward the tub.

"What kind of fool shit is this?" King murmured.

When Rawlings snapped the light back on, she had the top of her teddy pulled down around her waist, exposing a chest that made King instantly forget about the coolness of the water.

Rawlings approached him slowly, smiling the entire while. Pausing at one of the grocery bags, she reached in and pulled out a single ice cube. Pushing it slowly into her mouth, she licked it suggestively. Then, with an exaggerated swivel of her hips, she once again walked toward King.

He had about an hour to live, tops.

"Lean back, Lydell. I'm about to let you feel something probably no one ever has."

Rawlings smoothly knelt on the steps to King's bathtub, lowering her head until it was directly over his erect member. Pushing the ice cube partially out of her mouth, she slowly rubbed it around the tip of his penis in a circular motion, taking care that no skin-to-skin contact took place.

Then she spit the cube out. It bobbed toward King's feet.

"Close your eyes, Lydell," Rawlings said in a throaty voice. He did and felt the sensation of another cube swishing around sensitive nerve endings. He heard the rustle of a grocery bag crackling like lightning in the quiet.

Eyes closed, reclined against his tub, King smiled. He felt a third cold cube, then heard something sliding inside a bag and then the sound of little splashes in the water, along with the sensation of cold rocks falling against his penis and legs.

King opened his eyes to see Rawlings standing over the tub, emptying a plastic, five-pound bag of ice into the water and laughing her head off. In her left hand was a snub-nosed revolver pointed directly at his head! Both of her hands were encased in beige latex gloves.

"What the fuck are you doing?" he yelped. He tried to get up, but slipped back down into the tub.

"Lydell, if you try to get up, I'll blow your nuts off!" Rawlings said, suddenly serious. "If you think I'm joking, try it and see what happens."

Tossing the empty bag behind her, she bent down and turned the cold water on full blast. King's light brown eyes nearly bugged out of his head.

"That's cold!" he gasped, starting to shiver.

"No shit, Sherlock," Rawlings answered, reaching for another bag of ice while her gun remained locked on his forehead.

When King put his hands on the sides of the tub to hoist himself out, Rawlings cocked the trigger of her gun with an audible *click!*

"Your choice, Lydell," she said with eerie calm. "Because if you get out, muthafucka, I will cap you. Your choice."

"This joke has gone on long enough." An unmistakable quaver was in King's voice now.

"You see me laughing?" Rawlings practically flung the contents of another five-pound ice bag at him this time. *Plooop, plooop, plooop, plooop, plooop, plooop.* "DO YOU SEE ME LAUGHING?" she screamed, her face contorted with rage. "Did I laugh when you felt me up in the pharmacy all those times? HUH?"

She angrily yanked the top of her teddy back in place, shielding herself from being further violated by King's disgusting gaze. A shudder of revulsion went through her.

A third bag rained into the tub, followed immediately by a fourth and a fifth.

"You were expecting filet mignon?" Rawlings shrieked with laughter as she gleefully poured the sixth bag directly on King's head, then turned off the freezing water, which was starting to trickle through the tub's safety drain.

"What d-do you w-w-want?" King stuttered through clacking teeth, folding his arms in a futile attempt to stay warm. He had been enduring his ice bath for four minutes now.

Rawlings stopped in her tracks. "From you—nothing," she sneered. "Not one goddamned thing." She methodically emptied three more bags into the tub, all the while humming the tune to "Singin' in the Rain."

Numbness was starting to overtake King's legs and arms with lightning quickness. Alcohol makes the body dissipate heat quickly, hastening the onset of hypothermia. As Rawlings knew. Her experiences with Moore, Cooper and Hamilton had taught her everything she needed to know about hypothermia.

Strolling to the toilet, she pulled the seat cover down and sat on it, crossing her shapely legs. Still drawing a bead on King's right temple, she started glancing at her watch and drumming her fingers impatiently on the sink. She did that for five minutes.

"Well, looka here," Rawlings said, speaking in a voice thick with sarcasm as she got up. "We got a high-yaller niggah turning purple up in here. High-purple. It really doesn't become you, Lydell. Clashes with that sand-colored hair. And my, my—look at that itty-bitty dick! Were you planning on doing something with *that* little thing tonight, Lydell? Oh, dear!"

She poked out her bottom lip in mock disappointment, like a petulant child. Seeing that he was incapacitated, she turned around and bent over, poking her butt in his direction.

"Come and get it, BIG MAN!" she said in a low voice hoarse with outrage. She spun around to face him again. "WELL, THIS IS AS CLOSE AS YOU'LL EVER GET."

Slowly pulling out her tampon, Rawlings reared back and fired it at King with all her might. It caromed off his head and spun crazily through the air before smashing against the wall behind the bathtub.

King blinked uncomprehendingly, on the verge of sliding into shock. He tried to talk, but the air coming from his mouth made only a hissing sound. To his horror, he found that he could barely move and was growing more disoriented by the second.

"Hi, Lydell, wanna see something?" Now her voice dripped with facetious good cheer. Going into her overnight bag, Rawlings pulled out a three-inch-by-one-and-a-half-inch Confederate flag decal.

His eyelids were beginning to droop as the freezing water nudged him steadily toward unconsciousness and eventual cardiac arrest. Summoning herculean concentration and strength, King locked his eyes on Rawlings's and mouthed the word "You!"

"Yes, Lydell," she said, looking around for a guest towel to wipe away her fingerprints. "Little ol' me."

Wriggling out of her teddy, she starting putting her clothes back on. Then she gathered up the plastic bags on the floor and stuck them in her overnight bag. Ditto the champagne glasses and the two Asti bottles sitting on the dining room table.

Rawlings came back to the bathroom and, ignoring King, carefully reapplied her lipstick in the mirror. "Lydell!" she said cheerfully, looking at him in the mirror. His head had sunk onto his chest, and if he was breathing, she couldn't see it. "What's the matter, baby?" she asked, starting to giggle. "We're going to be late for our cocktail party!"

Picking her handgun up from the sink, Rawlings walked over to the tub and used the barrel of the snub-nosed .38 to push King's head back. Hard. It thudded against the back of the tub. Hypothermia had stilled Lydell King's heart.

"Oh, noooo, little boy blue! Where is the boy who attacks all the sheep? He's sitting in his bathtub—fast asleep. Ummpph!" Rawlings sat on the side of the tub doubled over, slapping her thighs and laughing until tears fell.

When she finished, she reached into the bottom of the tub—quickly, because the water was painfully cold—and opened the drain. She also wanted to limit her contact with water that had touched King's disgusting body.

Toweling off her right arm, Rawlings squatted directly in front of King. "Jerk-off, I have two things for you," she said, rummaging through her overnight bag. "First, this wonderful parting gift." She carefully peeled the backing off a Confederate flag decal and painstakingly attached it precisely to the center of his forehead.

"Second, I have a little secret for you, Lydell, baby." Holding her gun between her pinkie and her forefinger, she let it swing lazily in front of King's face. "The gun wasn't loaded, asshole!"

She took the guest towel and meticulously wiped every surface she had touched, including the refrigerator, the bathroom doorknob and the dining room table. Rawlings threw the towel in her overnight bag, got her coat out of the closet, snapped off her latex gloves and opened the front door to leave.

The phone began to ring.

Sorry, girlfriend, I got here first tonight. Lydell is out of commission, honey bunch.

CHAPTER FORTY-ONE

Whenever I reflect back on Phil Gardner's funeral, two images will always come barreling to my mind.

The first is of Scott Donatelli and Gardner's widow, Phyllis, locked arm in arm and clearly hurting, watching Gardner's gun-metal-gray casket slowly descend into the ground. Donatelli was actually crying harder than Mrs. Gardner—he was giving it up in Greenmount Cemetery like a black person, wailing and carrying on!

The second image is of Gardner's precious three-year-old granddaughter tossing a blue-and-red rubber ball up the church aisle right before her grandfather's casket was borne off to the graveyard. Life does go on, doesn't it?

That's what I keep reminding myself as I sit in my car in front of the forty-second pharmacy on my list, an Optima Pharmacy at the corner of Monument Street and Central Avenue, practically in the shadow of the Johns Hopkins Hospital medical complex.

I charge up to the front door of the Optima, glad to have something to occupy my mind other than Gardner's funeral. The Optima has that cruddy look and smell that franchises operating in Baltimore's inner city typically have.

At the rear of the store, a female Asian pharmacist and her young black female assistant are scurrying back and forth furiously as at least ten sisters, many of them holding sick children, glare furiously. They even have a little visual venom for me when I walk up to the counter, as though I was bogarting to the front of the line or something.

"We got a line in here," a particularly unattractive, nappy-headed woman barks at me.

"I'm not here for medicine—I need to talk to the pharmacist for a second," I tell her politely.

"You can still wait yo' ass at the back of the line!"

Rather than let this woman drag me to an ignorant place first thing in the morning, I lower my eyes and say nothing. I also don't move.

"You on Medicaid or state assistance?" the Asian pharmacist asks in a condescending tone, never bothering to look up.

"Neither," I respond evenly. "I was wondering if you could tell me if this woman works here." I whip out a picture of Cynthia Travers.

"No," the pharmacist says dismissively. "She no work here."

Nor does she work in twenty-three city pharmacies I visit before going to the *Herald* to write a story about Gardner, the hero cop. I'm in front of my computer, writing, when my phone rings, about seven o'clock. It's Donatelli.

"Come meet me at the Pratt Street condos," he says in a flat voice. "We've got another one."

Lydell King's body is in about a third of an inch of water, like Margaret Cooper's, and he's slumped down in the bathtub of his condo with one of those flags on his head. Though his eyes are open, King looks at peace.

Scott Donatelli is lecturing a police evidence technician in King's bathroom, obviously frustrated. Usually Donatelli looks youthful, but tonight his face is drawn and the shadows around his eyes make him look like a raccoon.

He doesn't nod or otherwise acknowledge my presence, even though he clearly sees me standing in the doorway of the bathroom.

"Who is this?" I ask after Donatelli wraps up his conversation.

He sweeps his hand through his greasy-looking black hair twice, looking irritable and edgy. He probably feels every eye in the city is on him right now, wondering why he can't catch this killer. That wouldn't be far off.

"Lydell Robert King," Donatelli says in a monotone. "He didn't go to work today and his mother sent one of his cousins over to check on him."

"How old is he, Scott?"

"Thirty-six years old. Look Darryl, I don't have time for a lot of questions right now, but I thought you'd want to know about this." Spoken with a brusqueness spawned by frustration.

I lay off Donatelli and spend a few minutes writing, describing King's pad in my notepad. On the tiled ledge beside the bathtub, just to the right of a small cactus in a blue ceramic flower pot, a white-and-red cylindrical object catches my eye. Huh?

"Hey, Scott, what is that?" I ask, pointing at it. "That can't be what I think it is—that a tampon?"

"You've got sharp eyes. Don't put that in your story, because it may be the first significant break we've had."

"Okay...just a few more questions, I promise." I throw out a few run-of-the-mill queries, saving the one I'm most interested in for last. "What kind of work did King do, Scott?" I hold my breath.

"He pushed drugs. He was a pharmacist."

I knew it! Now I'm positive that a woman is behind all these murders. "Hear me out on something," I say, stepping into the bathroom toward Donatelli.

"Don't come in here!" he yells. "The last thing I need is a compromised crime scene." He walks out of the bathroom, out of King's condo and into the hallway.

"Make this real, real quick, because I'm a little busy here," Donatelli says, his face getting red.

"Okay, here's the deal. You're not getting anywhere with your investigation. I'll bet any amount of money that King knew the woman I've been trying to find. Why don't you come with me to his pharmacy tomorrow when it opens and I'll show the employees there her picture. What have you got to lose?"

"An hour of wasted time that could be used finding the real goddamn killer," Donatelli snaps.

"Could it really hurt?" I ask in a quiet, cajoling voice. "Could it? If I'm wrong, I swear I'll never mention my theory again. Ever. That alone ought to make it worth the trip!"

I smile at Donatelli, who continues to grimace.

"He worked at a Drug-Mart on Rodgers and Park Heights avenues," he says with supreme irritation. "See you there at nine tomorrow morning."

He reenters King's condo and I rush downstairs to use a pay phone so I can alert the *Herald* of a fourth Confederate flag murder. Then I head back to work and write another story that winds up on the front page.

Someone has placed a shipping box beside my desk, which I open before I go home. Inside I find my missing-in-action laptop computer, which the Atlanta Police Department has kindly returned in good operating condition.

CHAPTER FORTY-TWO

So this is what it feels like to be unemployed. Damn good!

Brenda Rawlings had finally rid herself of "the cage," that ridiculously small work space where pharmacists and their assistants are forever scurrying around, bumping into each other. At least office workers could stretch their legs in the halls or visit other floors—Rawlings paced back and forth in her white pharmacy jacket like a polar bear in Baltimore's zoo.

Well, not anymore. She quit her job today—didn't even bother to go in. Just resigned over the phone. Thank you for the bereavement leave and please mail me a check for my unused vacation time. Later!

The Optima Pharmacy chain would do quite well without her. And God knew the drug companies would certainly keep making their billions. *I think they can manage to get by without Brenda Rawlings,* she thought, picking halfheartedly at two cold slices of pizza in her apartment.

She didn't have much of an appetite, nor had she gotten much sleep in the twenty-four hours since King's death.

Usually ultrafastidious about her personal hygiene, especially during her period, Rawlings hadn't bothered to wash today. It was just too much trouble. So she sat around in her jeans bare-chested, because a bra or a shirt would irritate her supersensitive breasts.

She'd been a buzzing high-voltage wire ever since leaving King's condo. *The power* had been liberating at first—now it was starting to imprison her. She couldn't eat or sleep or stop thinking death.

She had been in control at first, starting with Darcel Moore. He'd enticed Rawlings's mother into a bogus investment deal that had wiped out the old woman's life savings. Margaret Cooper had stolen the one true love of Rawlings's life just for the hell of it when they were in high school, long before Cooper had embraced a lesbian lifestyle. Melvin Hamilton, well, he was a case of wrong place, wrong time. Saying all the wrong things.

As for Lydell King, he had probably died too quickly and too humanely.

But now Brenda Rawlings was starting to feel as though she had to kill, as though it was linked to some primal need.

Well, that wouldn't pose a problem. There were plenty of people who had run roughshod over Brenda the Timid at some point or another. With nothing but time on her hands now, Rawlings started looking for paper and a pencil to make the list longer.

CHAPTER FORTY-THREE

Scott Donatelli and I are waiting at the front door of the Drug-Mart on the corner of Rodgers and Park Heights when the door opens at 9 A.M. Lydell King was very popular at the store, and the four employees opening for business are very subdued, still coming to grips with his death.

Donatelli identifies himself and asks if the pharmacist is present.

"He must be running a little late," replies an older, heavy-set black woman who appears to be the supervisor; she unlocks a metal barricade stretching across the front of the store. I identify myself and take Cynthia Travers's picture from my briefcase. "Ma'am, have you ever seen this woman?" I ask hopefully.

"Oh, that's Brenda," she says offhandedly. "She stopped working here about ten months ago. Nobody ever said why—she was here one day, gone the next."

I glance at Donatelli, who appears surprised. I've managed to place this Brenda woman in Atlanta at the time of the Confederate flag killing there, and I've established a link between her and a Confederate flag victim in Baltimore. There's no denying I'm onto something now.

"What is Brenda's last name?" Donatelli asks casually.

"Don't make me lie!" the woman says, pausing momentarily from pushing back the steel grate, which continues to vibrate and sway back and forth. "Rawlings! Brenda Rawlings. Real nice girl, too, real quiet. Never said much o' nothin' to nobody."

Why does that name ring a bell—Rawlings? Fred Rawlings, the kid who tossed me into traffic on Paca Street!

"Do you know where she works now?" Donatelli says firmly.

The woman thinks for a second, saying nothing. "Shondra, you knew her better than I did," she says finally. "Do you know where Brenda went?"

Shondra, a youthful-looking woman who looks like she belongs in high school, glances first at Donatelli, then at me. "Who did you say you were again?" she asks, spitting out the question with such violence it startles me.

"I'm a reporter with the *Herald*."

She regards me skeptically. "Brenda went to work for one of Optima's stores. I think the one downtown at Baltimore and Charles."

"Thanks."

I slowly walk away from the women, nodding discreetly for Donatelli to follow me. "You know that kid who tried to kill me before I left for Atlanta, Scott? His name is Fred Rawlings and I'll bet he's hooked up with this Brenda Rawlings some kind of way."

"I'll call down to headquarters, but first I'm going to see if I can get an address and a phone number." Donatelli quickly walks into the pharmacy where Lydell King worked, with me right on his heels.

"Girl, they got some slick-looking white cop and a black guy who says he's a reporter down here asking about you. You in trouble or sumpin'?" The minute Shondra looks up and sees us standing in front of her counter, she slams down the phone.

"Who was that?" Donatelli barks, oozing authority from every pore. "And you better tell me, because I can get this store's phone records, and if you're lying, you might go to jail for aiding a murderer."

"Brenda," the woman says in a squeaky little voice. "That was Brenda."

"Why in the hell did you call her?" Donatelli screams, appearing on the verge of losing it.

"'Cause she my girl!" Shondra says somewhat defiantly. Donatelli bends down in front of Shondra, and gets so close his nose practically touches hers.

"Lemme tell you somethin'," he says so quietly that I can barely hear, and I'm right beside him. "My partner *died* while trying to solve these murders. You'd better give me Brenda Rawlings's address and phone number *right now!* And if you call her after I leave, I'll personally see to it they put you *under* the jail."

Armed with Rawlings's address and phone number, and her picture from Atlanta, Donatelli drives over to her place, an apartment complex on Reisterstown Road in Northwest Baltimore.

I head toward Rawlings's new job, at the Optima Pharmacy in downtown Baltimore. When I get there, the pharmacist on duty, a middle-aged white guy, looks at me oddly.

"Who are you?" he asks suspiciously.

His suspicious expression is replaced by a confused look when I tell him. "What do you want with Brenda—if you don't mind my asking?"

"She may have a tie to the Confederate flag murders that have been taking place in the city."

He nods his head nonchalantly, as if his employees are always being suspected of that sort of thing. "She just quit yesterday," he says in a puzzled tone. "Never even came in, just quit over the phone. Good worker, a little on the shy side. Before she quit, she had been on bereavement leave—said she had a relative die out of town."

"In Georgia?"

"How did you know that?" he asks in amazement.

"It's a long story. Do you know where she is now?"

"I don't have the slightest idea. I have her phone number, if you want to call her."

As I leave the Optima Pharmacy where Rawlings used to work, I'd bet any amount of money that she's abandoned her apartment. And when I arrive at her complex, that's exactly the case. Donatelli and a bunch of cops are crawling all over her neat place, dismantling it bit by bit.

"We've already found a black overnight bag with some Victoria's Secret stuff in it and three packs of Confederate flag decals," Donatelli says elatedly, waving a search warrant. "As well as some champagne glasses and a couple of Asti Spumante bottles. We're going to see if they have any of the victims' prints on them. And look at this. We found these under her bed."

Inside a black three-ring binder, Rawlings has neatly clipped hundreds of magazine and newspaper articles about Wayne Williams, the sicko convicted of killing all those black kids in Atlanta.

Inside a smaller, red three-ring binder with a plastic cover, Rawlings has stenciled CODE RED: SATAN'S GUEST LIST.

There are nine pages after that, each focusing on a person Rawlings has apparently targeted for death. In many cases, a color photo of the person has been clipped from a yearbook or a newspaper and glued to that page.

And there's a little information about each person, an informal bio of sorts.

Darcel Moore is on page 1, along with information about his allegedly swindling Bonita Rawlings out of $23,313.91. Margaret Cooper and Lydell King are there, too, but Melvin Hamilton is missing.

Using a letter opener to flip the page so he doesn't leave prints, Donatelli turns to page 4 and I see—ME!

There are four asterisks beside my name, apparently indicating I'm a high-priority target. There's a large color picture of me receiving the key to the city in the wake of the NAACP bombing attempt. And my text has been underlined:

Hunting dress failed here, possibly gay! Busted Freddie's lip. Will definitely pay. Very, very special case. A bath won't cleanse this one. There's a need for a potent prescription. But as mortal blood flows through his veins, I will succeed.

Donatelli looks at me strangely. "What's that all about?"

"Long story, Scott. I'll tell you about it later. Right now, I've got a helluva story to write."

CHAPTER FORTY-FOUR

The Atlanta police confirmed today that Brenda Rawlings was in my room at the bed-and-breakfast. Plus, she's been made the primary suspect in all the Confederate flag killings and a warrant has been issued in Baltimore for her arrest.

All this has taken place since this morning—it's about six o'clock in the afternoon now.

In addition, Fred Rawlings has confirmed that Rawlings is his aunt, but his lawyers are keeping mum about his pitching me into Paca Street. In fact, he pleaded not guilty at his arraignment hearing.

I don't feel comfortable with Yolanda and Jamal in the house while Rawlings is out there seeing red and likely gunning for yours truly. But Yolanda isn't helping matters by refusing to leave the house. The more I beg her to take Jamal and go somewhere else until I can get home, the harder she digs in.

Her response to the threat has been to pull out the handgun we've hidden in our house, take the safety lock off it and tote the thing around like Annie Oakley. And she says LaToya is over at the house, too, so she's not worried about a thing.

Having seen what Brenda Rawlings is capable of, I'm positive that she could kill Yolanda, Jamal and LaToya without batting an eyelash.

Yolanda's independence is one of the things that attracted me to her, but there are times when it's one of the characteristics I like the least. She sounded miffed and huffy the second time I called back to check on her well-being, but frankly, I don't care. I'm going to keep right on checking until I get home.

Meanwhile, my own phone won't stop ringing as I try to write my story. And each time it's been a reporter on the other end, insistently seeking a quote for some media outlet. After twelve calls, one right after the other, I irritatedly log off from my computer terminal and walk to the opposite side of the newsroom. I plop myself down at another reporter's desk, log on to his computer terminal and continue writing.

After about an hour and a half, by which time I'm wrapping up, I check my messages just to make sure the cops didn't call with a new development. Like Rawlings getting arrested or something.

There are four more aggravating messages from reporters before I get to one that makes my heart skitter around inside my rib cage.

"Yo, what up, dawg?" Mad Dawg says breathlessly. "Can't talk loud, boy, 'cause I got company in the next room. But a honey came by my crib tonight who's the BA-ZOMB! And she wants to give up dem drawers bad, kid! LaToya is at your place with Yolanda, and I think they're going shopping. Gotta go, kid, but this honey says she knows you. Her name is Cynthia Travers. Peace, out."

I frantically call Dawg's phone number, which rings and rings until his answering machine picks up.

"Dawg!" I scream. "If you can hear me, please pick up the phone." What I don't realize is that he has one of those answering services you get through the phone company—there's no way he can monitor his calls.

Three thoughts crowd their way into my mind at the same instant: Dawg is having sex with that crazy woman, he's left his apartment or he's left this earth.

Trying to crowd that last possibility out of my brain, I dial another number; my right index finger is a blur as it flies across the keypad. Yolanda picks up. "Baby, just listen, okay? Call the cops over to Mad Dawg's. If LaToya has a key, ask her to bring it so she can open the door—but not before the cops get there. I think the Confederate flag killer is in his apartment."

Then I hang up and race over to Dawg's apartment on Hillen Road, near Morgan State University. I run every red light and break every speed limit, hoping I do get stopped by a policeman for once. I don't, but I do manage to make it from downtown to Dawg's place in just ten minutes.

There's not a police cruiser in sight, although I do see Yolanda's car. She and LaToya are anxiously pacing the sidewalk as Jamal waits in the car. LaToya is sobbing.

"Where are the cops?" I ask Yolanda.

"They haven't gotten here," she replies, looking wild-eyed and distraught.

"Did you bring the gun?"

"Yes."

"Let me have it."

"What are you going to do?" Yolanda asks, hesitating before she opens her purse and hands me the nine-millimeter. I bought it when Mark Dillard and his crew went on trial for the attempted NAACP bombing, because I kept getting death threats like nobody business. I have yet to take the thing to a shooting range and fire it.

"You two go back to the car with Jamal," I shout over my shoulder, before entering the front door and starting to sprint up three flights of stairs to Dawg's garden apartment.

"Like hell," LaToya says, running after me.

After LaToya and I reach the fourth floor, I stand outside Dawg's door for several seconds, breathing hard and trying to see if I can hear anything over the sound of my pulsating heart in my ears. Other than the muffled singing of Luther Vandross, I don't hear a thing.

"Lemme have the key," I tell LaToya under my breath.

The same key opens both locks and I push the door open very, very slowly. Unlike on television, where armed people make their entrance with weapons pointed to the sky, I have mine held out in front of me with both hands, ready to pull the trigger. As jumpy as I am right now, anything or anyone that makes a sudden move into my field of vision is likely to get blasted. I hope this isn't one of Dawg's practical jokes.

I look at LaToya, put a finger to my lips and quickly tiptoe into Dawg's living room. The Luther CD is a good sign—Dawg must have been listening to it in the last few minutes or so. I'm glad it's on for another reason—it nicely masks the sound of my footsteps.

"Don't you remember you told me you love me, baby?" Luther croons as I move toward the bathroom door, which is cracked, allowing light to stream out into the dark hallway.

Taking one hand off the gun, I quickly push the door open. In the stark glare of a bare sixty-watt lightbulb near the medicine cabinet, I saw exactly what I prayed not to see all the way over here.

My best friend is reclined on the bottom of his bathtub, underwater, with his dreadlocks flowing around his head and his eyes open. He's under a good two to three inches of ice cubes. At six-foot-four, Dawg can no way fit entirely into the tub—his legs are bent at the knees, which jut out of the water.

"Dawg!"

I lay my gun on the floor and plunge my hands into the painfully cold water. I grab Dawg under his armpits and hoist his stiff, frigid body out of the tub and gently lay him on the bathroom floor.

Then I pick up the handgun again and go through the rest of his apartment.

A hurried search of the kitchen and the laundry room turns up nothing. No one is hiding in the laundry room or the closets. The last place anyone could be is the bedroom, whose door is wide open.

Entering slowly, ready to fire off a shot, I immediately spot a woman lying on the bed with her back to the door. She's wearing a gold teddy whose material is so flimsy I can see right through it. A nearly empty bottle of Asti Spumante is on the nightstand beside the bed, along with a pill bottle that's turned on its side.

"If you move, I swear to God I will shoot you!" I scream, advancing slowly toward the woman. "Turn around slowly and put your hands over your head." Whoever it is has chosen to ignore me.

"Darryl!" a female voice yells out behind me. Before I can even think, I'm pivoting and aiming toward the door. Right at LaToya's torso—how I managed to avoid shooting her is something I will never understand.

I snap back around, giving the woman on the bed my full attention. "Stay out of here, LaToya. Go in the bathroom and lock the door. Do CPR on Mad Dawg."

Walking back to the bed, I keep the nine-millimeter pointed at the woman in the teddy and roughly jerk her left shoulder toward me. It's Brenda Rawlings. Her eyes are closed and her breathing is very, very shallow.

There's a sudden commotion in the hallway and two cops brandishing their weapons rush into the bedroom. "Drop the gun," one of them says, aiming his weapon at me.

"I'm going to squat because I don't want it to go off, okay?"

"DO IT!"

Flexing my knees in slow motion, I sink to the ground and let my gun drop about six inches. It falls into the padded carpet with a dull thud. I remain on my knees as one of the officers snatches the gun off the floor, then tends to Rawlings.

"God, please spare my best friend. He doesn't always do the right things, but he has a good heart." I make the sign of the cross, something I haven't done since I was a little boy and my parents made me attend the Catholic church every Sunday.

From the bathroom comes the scalp-tingling sound of LaToya's anguished screams as she scuffles with police officers trying to help Mad Dawg.

CHAPTER FORTY-FIVE

It's been touch and go with Mad Dawg. He was taken to Ida B. Wells Hospital, where they were able to get his heart restarted, but he hasn't regained consciousness. According to the doctors, he's in a deep coma that could last a week or months—there's no way of telling.

I'm standing at his bedside right now, staring down at him as a machine takes care of his breathing. The doctors don't trust his body to perform that elementary function just yet.

The machine seems to magnify the sound of every breath, giving it a ghastly loudness that reverberates through his intensive-care room. Dawg's eyes are closed and he's not looking particularly peaceful or pained. He's just...there.

"Dawg, you gotta get out of here, man." I say quietly, laying my hand on his cool forehead. As has been the case since he got here, there's no reaction, no eyeball rolling, nothing. Dawg's loud Eddie Murphy laugh used to embarrass the hell out of me, but I would give anything to hear it now. It would be music.

Brenda Rawlings died not long after arriving at the hospital. The doctors said she had enough barbiturate in her system to kill a horse, and had combined that with alcohol. Ordinarily

I would be out digging, interviewing people, trying to make sense of the enigma that was Brenda Rawlings in order to write about it for the *Herald*.

But I'm not in the proper frame of mind to return to work yet. I called Florence Newsome and she understood instantly. She told me to take as much time off as I need, that I had already broken the Confederate flag story and basically solved the murders. That I was a hero.

How come I can't make my friend do something as simple as sitting up in his bed and talking?

Mad Dawg's first twenty-four hours in the hospital were absolute torture. The doctors leveled with LaToya, Yolanda and me by letting us know it was fifty-fifty whether he lived or died. Other than grabbing a sandwich and going to the bathroom, I really haven't left Mad Dawg's room. Somehow, I know he can sense my presence. I know he can feel me trying to will the life force not to leave his body. He needs that right now.

LaToya hasn't left, either, which tells me a lot about Yolanda's sister.

There was one time about three in the morning when a low heartbeat and blood pressure triggered alarms on the equipment Dawg's hooked up to, scaring the shit out of me and LaToya.

But now something tells me that Dawg is out of the woods. At least in terms of whether he'll survive tonight and the next day. When, or if, he comes out of that coma is anybody's guess. But being an optimist, I sense he'll beat that, too.

"Dawg, can you hear me, man? Come on, stop fooling around."

What I see next could be my imagination, or just a manifestation of wishful thinking. But I could swear the corners of his mouth gave a barely perceptible upward twitch, in what could only be interpreted as a smile.

"Can you hear me, man?" I ask excitedly.

LaToya is immediately at my side. "What's wrong, Darryl?" She grabs Dawg's hand and squeezes it hard.

"It looked like his mouth moved, like he was trying to smile."

"I believe you, Darryl," LaToya says, squeezing my hand, too. "I believe you."

"LaToya, I'm going home tonight, to sleep in my own bed. Call me if anything happens...but I'm sure everything is going to be fine."

"Tell Sis I said hi," LaToya says, kissing me on my cheek.

On my way home I stop at Mondawmin Mall to buy something that's been on my mind for several months now. I can finally afford it.

When I get home I kiss Yolanda on the lips, hug Jamal, take off my clothes and collapse in bed, dead to the world.

CHAPTER FORTY-SIX

Brenda Rawlings had a malignant tumor growing in her brain, a common category of brain tumor known as astrocytoma, according to the state medical examiner. Whether that was the reason for her murderous behavior, only God knows. But it was growing in the part of the brain that governs emotions, so it was likely the cause of her actions.

The one person who knows for sure carried that knowledge to the grave.

Scott Donatelli called to tell me about Rawlings at 6:40 in the morning. He also thanked me—for what, I'm not sure. Because I didn't go after Rawlings as a personal favor to him. Not knowing what else to say, I merely said, "You're welcome."

He's really been getting hero treatment now that the killings have been pinned on Rawlings. Which is cool with me—I hope he gets a promotion out of it, too. Because the Confederate flag murders weren't something I tackled for acclaim or simply to do a job. It ran a lot, lot deeper than that.

I feel like going to work today, but first I'll swing past Ida B. Wells to see how my boy is progressing.

Finally, some good news out of the hospital. Mad Dawg looks the exact same to my untrained eye. But the doctors say he's beginning to react to stimuli like being pinched and having lights flashed in his eyes, a very good sign.

LaToya is curled up in a chair in his hospital room, sound asleep. "Yo, man, I'll be back in a few," I tell Dawg, who I'm convinced is listening to everything I say. "But first, I have to go to the tenth floor and take care of something."

The elevator door opens on the tenth floor just as Yolanda pushes her food tray into a patient's room. I loiter near the elevator and duck around the corner every time she enters and leaves a room to deliver breakfast. When she has no more trays on her cart and is just about to enter a service elevator to get more food, I jog down the hall and follow her into the elevator right before the door closes. No one else is in it except us.

"Darryl! What are you doing up here!" she exclaims.

Jamming my left hand into my pocket, I grab Yolanda's hand and get down on one knee. "You've been giving of yourself to others all morning," I say, the words magically appearing from nowhere. "Because that's the kind of person you are—nurturing, kind, selfless. You've added a dimension to my life—you and Jamal—that I never knew could exist. You make me feel things, and give of myself, like no other woman has. Will you marry me, Yolanda?"

Taking my left hand out of my pocket, I present her with a one-and-a-half-carat diamond engagement ring. I'm glad to be down on one knee. That way, Yolanda is clueless how badly my knees are shaking.

She just stands there with her mouth open, on unsteady legs of her own. Then the tears start flowing, but no sound leaves her mouth.

"Darryl, get off your knees," she manages to say between sobs. "Oh, Darryl!" She puts her arms around me and hugs me hard, not stopping even after several other people enter the elevator.

When her floor arrives, she pushes her cart off, still without having given me an answer.

"Well?"

She pauses for what seems like an entire day. "Darryl, I would be honored to be your wife and to share my life with you. But I can't accept your proposal—not now. Your best friend is in a coma. I don't think you're thinking clearly right now. I want to make sure your proposal isn't coming from some sense of loss. Does that make sense to you, baby?"

It makes perfect sense. And it brings me even closer to Yolanda, because I know a lot of women who would have taken that carat and a half and tipped happily into the sunset. But proposing to Yolanda isn't something that just popped into my head—I've been mulling this one over for about half a year.

"You haven't heard the last of Darryl Billups," I tell Yolanda before tasting her sweet tongue. "I love you, Yolanda. Nothing that happens with my friends or relatives will change the way I feel for you."

When I get back to Mad Dawg's room, LaToya, the doctors and the nurses are all gathered around his bed, ecstatic. His eyes still aren't open, but he's feebly grabbing people's fingers and giving two weak squeezes for yes, one for no.

Pushing my way through the crowd around his hospital bed, I grab Mad Dawg's right hand. "Whazzup, boy! This is Darryl. Can you hear me?"

The fingers on his right hand barely move twice.

"Do you want me to go out and bring you back a beer, kid?"

Two more weak squeezes have me and everyone else in the room rocking with laughter, delighted by this unexpected sign of recovery.

"Have you learned anything from this, Dawg?"

Ever so slowly, he opens his eyes and looks around his hospital room. Dawg then gazes directly at me and, chuckling quietly, fires off a burlesque wink.

"Mad Dawg!"

ABOUT THE AUTHOR

The son of two Baltimore public school teachers, Blair S. Walker used to entertain himself in elementary school by writing short stories. The practice was frowned upon by instructors who wanted Walker to pay attention in class rather than secretly heed his muse. After serving in the Army as a Korean linguist, Walker attended the University of Maryland and worked as an intern reporter with the *Baltimore Sun*. Hired by the *Orlando Sentinel* after college, Walker was fired after six months by an editor who disparagingly noted that Walker's writing ability was marginal at best! A former financial writer with *USA Today*, Walker has been an editor with *New York Newsday* and the *Washington Post*, and a newsman with the Associated Press. The author of three novels featuring investigative reporter Darryl Billups, Walker holds a University of Maryland J.D. degree and currently lives in South Florida, where he's pursuing a lifelong dream of learning to fly helicopters.

Made in the USA
Charleston, SC
26 June 2011